JUMBO

GABRIELLE LORD

JUMBO

THE BODLEY HEAD
LONDON

For my parents, Gwen and John Butler

British Library Cataloguing
in Publication Data
Lord, Gabrielle
Jumbo
I. Title
823[F] PR9619.3.L6

ISBN 0 370 30703 8

Printed in Great Britain for
The Bodley Head Ltd
30 Bedford Square, London, WC1B 3RP
by Redwood Burn Ltd, Trowbridge

Photoset by Rowland Phototypesetting Ltd
Bury St Edmunds, Suffolk
First published in 1986

I

For the rest of her life, Verity would suffer remorse. Not only because of the old guilt that, unresolved, had undermined her life for so long, but because of that particular Christmas. In time, the earliest torment would ease, but bitter ambushes of conscience and imagination would continue to attack her. A child in despair and a good man dead—if only, she'd think, if only I'd read the first letter properly. If only I hadn't been angry with Richard that morning and thrust the first one aside. She'd stand with her back to the window, leaning against the sink and staring at the kitchen table where the torn envelope had lain, its contents neglected. It hadn't been until the arrival of the second letter that she'd become frightened, but by then it was too late, and the first one had disappeared days ago.

So she had stood that morning, waiting for the kettle to boil, in their comfortable home as the early sun shone through the windows, already hot. She made tea, buttered toast, and listened to Richard stamping around the bedroom, frantically looking for a clean shirt.

'You must have one,' she called. 'It's got to be in there.'

'It's not.'

She ignored the anger in his voice, steeled herself against going and looking for it. She set plates and cups on the table and sat down, pouring herself some tea. She spread toast with marmalade. Shortly Richard came in wearing yesterday's shirt and glaring at her. He sat at the table and poured tea, picked up the newspaper and studied it. Verity ate calmly, pretending not to notice his mood.

'Toast?'

He shook his head. She didn't persist and after a while

5

took the neglected second piece herself. Just as she was finishing it, Richard looked up from the newspaper.

'Any toast left?'

'Not now.' She chose her words carefully, avoiding pronouns. 'More,' she said, 'will need to be made.'

He glanced at the clock, a frying pan with hands, on the wall.

'Too late now. I'll have to go.'

'O K.' Her voice was neutral.

'Oh,' he continued, 'have you decided yet?'

'About what?' She knew quite well, but was unprepared and needed time.

'About Christmas. About whether we're going to stay with Natalie and Tony. I'll have to know soon. Tony was asking me again yesterday.'

Verity looked out of the kitchen window. Dew was rising in steam from the brown lawn, and the flowers were burnt from yesterday's westerly. Christmas with the Jansens at their resort unit on the Gold Coast; two weeks of polite small talk with Natalie while Tony and Richard got drunk and argumentative every day and pretended to be fishermen. No. She didn't want to do that again, but to say so now would cause painful and useless argument.

'I'll let you know very soon.'

'How soon?' he persisted.

'Soon soon.'

'What is it you want to do anyway?'

'I was thinking of getting away for a week or two by myself.'

'By yourself? But you've never done that.'

'No. Exactly.'

Richard stood up, his good-looking features pulled into a frown. He pulled on his coat, felt in his pocket for the car keys and drew out a letter.

'Oh. I forgot. This came for you yesterday.'

One of Richard's most irritating habits was collecting the mail and holding it in his pocket or in the glove box of his car for days. She put her hand out for it. The writing on the

6

envelope was strange to her, childish. Without interest, she tore it open, barely glanced at the body of it, noting the tiny circles that were used to dot the i's.

'Hi, Miss,' it started and the suburb of the address was even further west than the one where they lived. It was signed oddly: the word 'Jumbo' in inverted commas. She shoved it back into the envelope. She had no enthusiasm for the moment to devote to an ex-pupil.

'Where do you want to go to? By yourself?'

Verity shrugged. 'I really haven't thought that far yet. I thought I'd spend a few days with Mum. She hasn't been well.'

'You can count me out of that.'

She looked at him in silence, not saying the obvious, and he left quickly and without saying goodbye. She listened to his car pull out of the driveway and the angry screech of his tyres as he accelerated away. He taught at the high school, but her school was only a few blocks away, the primary. She no longer took her car but enjoyed the walk in the morning and usually got a lift on her return home in the heat of the afternoon.

She sat on for a while, enjoying her tea. It was almost over, the last term of the school year. Exams were finished and both teachers and children were enduring that silly season of the last few weeks devoted to half-hearted attempts on next year's work, and the making of papery Christmas craft. Her class, usually well behaved, were bored and restless by this time. Their sunburnt arms stuck to the desks when they leaned on them, and white pages soon became grubby. It was a stinker of a summer. She crushed out her half-smoked cigarette and dumped the plates and cups in the sink. She noticed the letter again and put it on top of the fridge with some bills and receipts. Odd, she thought to herself, I can't remember ever having taught anyone called Jumbo.

Richard and Verity's house was one in an estate in Sydney's western suburbs, bulldozed from straggly bush several years before. Sydney, like life itself, had grown from the sea, the

Pacific and the mouth of the Parramatta River. Even the hottest days in Sydney are refreshed by the sea-borne easterlies. The river valley goes back from the coast, through a plain for about forty miles, until it meets the walls of the Great Dividing Range. These are ancient mountains, deceptively worn, so that they appear young and rounded and exceptionally blue. They form the end and rim of the hot Cumberland Plain. A few miles from the sea the easterly breeze is no longer felt and in the summer the heat increases. Twenty-five miles from the coast the air is still and oppressive, fumed with car exhausts and the spouts of industry. Forty miles inland, under the shimmering rim of the mountains, the heat can be desperate. The mountains throb in the background, gathering up and absorbing the sun's power, radiating it back on to the plain where the houses of the outer western suburbs cluster. Land is cheaper out here, forty miles from the Harbour. The householders plant narrow pencil pines and wall their homes with glass. Huge picture windows glare out on to the black tar, and slow bubbles swell on the roads. The heat ricochets from the mountains and the black roads straight back through the picture windows. Night falls, but the houses stay hot for hours as the mountains radiate the enormous stored heat of the day. Bush fires burn for days up there, so that you might almost think that the sandstone of the ridges has burst into spontaneous flame. There are a couple of cooler hours till sunrise starts the process again—people can finally get to sleep, waking drained a few hours later to have tepid showers, forced breakfasts and thence go to work.

Richard had insisted on air-conditioning, so that their living room and bedroom, even in midsummer and at great expense, was a similar temperature to Sydney at night. It was a great relief to walk into the house after teaching all afternoon in a portable classroom steaming with thirty-four sticky, gritty and cranky kids. It was pleasant to sit in the lounge with a drink, feet on the cool glass-topped table, or to sprawl on the cream woollen carpet—the sort of carpet only childless couples have.

8

It could be worse, Verity thought, I could be living at Avondale where this morning's letter had come from; an area infested with wreckers' yards, used car lots decorated with dirty bunting. On the one- and two-acre lots in Avondale, the people had built their weatherboard homes and battled with the burrs and clay to make gardens. Dusty fowls scratched in the dirt under abandoned car bodies. Even the eucalypts out there were stunted, scorched by the westerly. As well as the heat and the ugliness, she thought, the outer west was bursting with children and adolescents, and adolescents having more children. Fat girls in tent dresses pushed fat babies in prams through the air-conditioned glitz of the shopping complex.

In the older, cooler central Sydney suburbs, you didn't see children playing any more, except for the pretty dark-haired rogues of the inner, undesirable few miles. Aboriginal, Lebanese, Greek; beautiful children who lived in either the stalags of the Housing Commission, or the tiny patched houses on the street, with their windows an arms' length from the passers-by. Once every few years a woman, spoiled and protected by the Housing Commission, living on a low rate of rent from her pension and with only a few children to worry about, hurls herself from the top floor of the crowded towers in total disregard for the responsibilities of motherhood. The stain is hosed away, the children taken into welfare and the building simmers for a few days, then settles down again. At least they have the easterly, Verity thought wryly. She missed Sydney badly, but she and Richard, despite their double salary, would find it almost impossible to buy their way back again, and, she had to admit, she'd grown half fond of the wide garden where she enjoyed sitting in the temperate months, reading or writing letters. Or sometimes just blindly staring, aching for her daughter taken from her all those years ago, and who would be celebrating her sixteenth birthday somewhere in Australia on Christmas Day.

She went straight to the staff room, divided into work stations for individual teachers. Books towered untidily on

9

the several desks and already ashtrays were filling at the smoking end of the room.

'Good morning, Helen,' she greeted her friend.

'Nothing much good about it,' with a smile that belied the words, 'except that there are only eight such others to go.'

'Coffee?'

'No, thanks. I haven't time.'

Verity gathered up her programme and the books she needed for the morning's teaching and went to her classroom. It was already absurdly decorated with paper reindeer hanging in mobiles, and a snowy Christmas tree stood at the end of the room. She dusted chalk from her desk and opened all the windows. The air outside was still and hot, and in the west, creamy cumulus were building up behind the hazy mountains. There might be a storm, she hoped, perhaps hail. She sat at her desk checking the programme. She had tests to mark so she chalked some maths for class on the blackboard. The bell rang and she hurried to the playground to escort her class inside. They came quietly enough; a few pushes on the steps, and a few playful prods and giggles. They stood behind their chairs and greeted her, then flopped noisily into place with loud scrapings of chairs and desks. She had grouped them into three circles round their tables. 'All right, you delightful bunch of toads. I'm sorry for what I'm about to do to you, but you'll notice some laughably easy puzzles on the board.'

There was a murmur of resentment; no one was fooled. Verity raised a hand. 'And,' she continued, 'if you want to know how you went in your history tests, you had best let me finish marking them in peace.'

They saw the sense of her suggestion and flapped open exercise books, sharpened pencils and set to work good-naturedly enough. She had long ago forsworn the special teacher's voice that so many of her colleagues used. She spoke to her class as if they were human and they responded with appreciation. She'd had this class last year when they were fifth grade; she'd grown to like them, and they liked her.

There were one or two she would rather be without, but after two years she'd learned to manage even them.

'Miss?'

She looked up from her work.

'Graham Shandly has taken my red pencil and won't give it back.'

'Give it back, Graham.'

'It's mine, Miss. Carleen took it last week and said it was hers.'

'O K. Bring it up here and I'll mind it till we sort things out.' Graham reluctantly laid the disputed pencil on her desk.

At recess, she shared coffee and a cigarette with Helen. The older woman, Verity thought, was probably the best teacher she had worked with, enthusiastic, generous, and dedicated to her job in a way that often made Verity feel a dilettante.

'Helen?'

'Mmm?' The quick brown eyes looked up from a book.

'Can you remember anyone called Jumbo? Someone I taught?'

Helen shook her head. 'No. Not Jumbo. That's a new one to me.'

'It would have been three, maybe four years ago.'

'No. I can't remember any name remotely like that.'

'It's just that I had a letter this morning from someone I've taught and that's how it was signed.'

'Perhaps you've just forgotten.'

This time it was Verity's turn to shake her head. 'No. You might forget to think of them for ages, but you only have to hear the name and they practically rise in front of you. I'd never forget someone called Jumbo.'

But it seemed that she had.

'O K. You can start packing up now.'

The children banged and crashed their cases on the desks, throwing books and papers in. The classroom was permeated with that special smell of school cases; a mixture of bananas, pencil-shavings and musty paper. Verity felt a small trickle of sweat run down her right arm. Outside, the cumulus were dissipating ahead of a hot westerly. The storm hadn't come and the air was stifling. As she watched, a police car pulled into the grounds. It parked near the Admin block and a uniformed man got out, pushed his shirt into his trousers, adjusted the squat, leather holster on his hip and started to walk towards her classroom. An unpaid traffic fine? Surely they wouldn't come to the school? The kids had noticed and were making jokes.

'Hey, Miss! You've had it. For cruelty to kids.'

'Hey, Chook! Remember the job on the canteen?'

'Oor, bullshit!'

'Miss, Chook knocked off ten Kitkats when Mrs Dunn wasn't—'

'No, I never!'

'You did so!'

'You shut up, Carleen Monigan!'

'Belt up, all of you!' Verity went to the door and met the police officer. He was a stocky fellow, tightly built and not much taller than she was.

'Mrs Unicombe?'

'Yes.'

'I want to have a word with you. About the kids.'

For a wild moment she thought he meant her class, then she remembered it was Detective Sergeant Bennett, father of Michelle in her class and a younger girl in Helen's grade.

The bell rang and the class erupted.

'I'll dismiss the children and be with you.'

She turned back to them. 'Settle down. Don't go on like drongoes just because the bell's gone.'

But they were already wild, excited by the uniformed man and going home.

'I'm going to be a policeman, Miss.'

'Me too! I'm going to be a highway patrol man and go real fast.'

She longed to yell at them, but stood behind her desk until they were reasonably quiet.

'OK. Homework.'

They groaned horribly. She cast about for something to give them. 'For your homework, just read one thing. One thing from anywhere and tell me about it on Monday.'

'A comic?'

'Anything.'

'I'm going to read—'

'I didn't ask you what you were going to read, Anthony Upton,' she yelled, hating herself as she did. 'Just read something. Anything.'

'A porno book!'

'Yes. If you can. And tell me all about it.' That was a shocking blunder, and she knew it even as the words were forming. Whistles and cheers erupted from the boys and the girls looked around fearfully.

'Shut up!' she roared, and they did. 'Try and walk out of the room without too much mayhem. Have a good weekend.'

'You too, Miss.'

'Thanks.'

'See you.'

'See you.'

They shambled out of the room and it seemed immediately cooler without them. Outside, the oppressive sky that couldn't rain pressed down, incandescent grey.

'Sorry to trouble you like this.'

'No trouble.'

He fiddled with his belt buckle, looking down.

'The wife's left me. That's why Michelle hasn't been to school this week. And Raquelle. I don't know what to do. They're upset.' He was incompetent to explain his tragedy and its results.

'I see,' she said uselessly.

'So I thought I'd better tell you. You'd be wondering what's happened to them. I didn't feel like writing it in a note.'

'No.'

'So I thought I'd better tell you.'

They stood awkwardly together under the glaring grey sky and the sergeant's face darkened. 'She ran away with the tennis coach.' He spat the last two words out as if they were poison.

'Thanks for telling me, Detective Sergeant.'

'Tom,' he replied. She smiled and nodded.

'I won't take up any more of your time.'

'I'll do what I can about the girls.'

'Look,' the uniformed man said. 'I'm pretty hopeless at the moment. Do you think we could meet—maybe after work? I don't know what to do about the girls. You might be able to—well—if I could just talk with you.'

'Yes,' she heard herself answer. She felt uncomfortable and tried to slow her words down. 'Yes. We could do that. Although I'm not sure what help I could offer.' His relief showed in his face. Did he think, wondered Verity, that because she was a teacher and trained to deal with children that she had some secret knowledge that would be of use to him? The idea made her smile and this softened the awkwardness between them.

'Good-oh. I'll be in touch then. Goodbye, Mrs Unicombe.'

He turned and she watched him get back into his car, shoulders hunched, pain and anger in every step he took. She locked the classroom and went home.

She let herself into the house. Immediately, the cool, conditioned air embraced her sticky body. She dumped her bag, still heavy with unmarked tests, on the kitchen table. Poor Michelle, she was thinking. A nice kid with wide eyes and short, thick hair, and a way of looking through the hair that could be utterly disarming. Poor bloody kids. They don't understand about grown-ups. And Tom Bennett himself left in anger and confusion. When someone as all-pervasive as a wife leaves, it must be very hard for a man, she thought. The sudden absence of the person responsible for all the invisible threads that knit a household and a family together, as unnoticeable and as important as the air that you breathe, must be a blow unimaginable to a woman. Verity remembered having briefly met Mrs Bennett at last year's fête; a pretty woman with wide eyes, but already there was that lack of lips so noticeable out here, as if constant and grim determination was the only manner of living.

Verity went to her mirror and studied her own face. What might it tell an observer? It was smooth, lightly tanned with fairly regular features. I'm all neutral tones, she thought to herself; fawns and beiges and mushroom rose. My eyes are no real colour at all but some neutral, soft khaki. Even my hair seems to lack colour, an absence of brownness, rather than brown. It's a nothing face with nothing colours.

She took a cold drink from the refrigerator, kicked off her sandals and collapsed into a chair. The old guilt was coiling around somewhere between her diaphragm and her pelvis. Was she better, or any worse, she wondered, for having abandoned her child before the child could know and love her? Did the child carry the stigma of her sorrow with every waking hour?

She discarded the lemonade, wanting something stronger. She poured a whisky and water and sat, looking out at the garden. Outside, the cicadas drilled in cadences. Sometimes they fell silent together, but one lone sentinel could recall the choir immediately. She looked at the backyard where the overgrown native trees crowded what was supposed to have been a lawn. A chair and table out there reminded her of all the times she'd sat there in the cooler months, hoping that the peace of the garden would help her turmoil.

Every year, she was thinking, the pain recreated itself towards Christmas, as Perdita's birthday approached. It was, she thought, like an infection with a yearly cycle. Most of the time it was a dull ache, only aroused by a sudden jolt or knock, but one that grew as Christmas approached every year. In sixteen years it had not improved. In every bath or shower that she took, her brown nipples reminded her of motherhood. There was still the faintest line from navel to pubis that also marked the passage of a child.

She sipped her drink, recoiling from the taste of spirits.

15

She must think of something else. What would she do if she didn't go away with Richard? She had no real plans. At the back of her mind was the vaguest of ideas—to trace her daughter. There were ways of doing this. But why now? What was happening around her that the desire was becoming urgent? Was it the approach of middle age, the sudden realization that she would never be a mother again? In earlier years, she imagined, there had been at least the ghosts of possible children between Richard and herself. They had not been important, but they'd been there. The large backyard had been chosen as a place for children to grow and play in; the spare bedroom and the study had once been thought of as potential nurseries.

She sighed. So many layers of rationalization to penetrate before she could know or trust herself. She spoke aloud, irritably shifting from one chair to another. 'I don't want kids because I don't want kids, full stop.' It didn't satisfy. Despite herself, she found herself wondering how Michelle's mother could leave her children, before she could check her own self-righteousness. Helen had once told her that if you keep increasing the height of the hurdles, you'll finally trip the horse, no matter how courageous it is. And it is often the bravest and most spirited of us who fall last and hardest, she'd added.

Her own mother, Verity thought, had once been high-spirited, but the early death of her husband, the awful jobs she'd taken in schools and hospitals, had worn her down. Her mother's own bitterness had been her poisoning. No, she decided, she would not think of her mother. It only angered her.

2

Lisa walked to the Employment Office. Today she'd try really hard, she thought. She had her best blouse and skirt on, and even though they hurt her feet she wore her best pair of shoes. As she passed a shop window, she glanced at her reflection. Her new confidence died. Even in her best things she looked somehow run-down and shabby. Her good blouse had lost its crispness; her skirt sagged round her narrow buttocks. She nearly collided with another girl.

'Sorry,' she gasped. The other didn't reply; just threw back her glossy hair and walked on. Her clothes were smart, and Lisa could tell she had a job.

In the Employment Office, she looked at the job boards. She'd long since given up trying for office jobs. All those were in the city anyway, and she was no competition for the well-dressed city girls. Employers lost interest when they heard the long-distance telephone bleeps—a dead give-away that the caller lived over forty miles distant. The rare local clerical job that did appear was gone within minutes, and the employer had his or her pick of the local cream. And cream Lisa knew she was not. So she looked at the sales jobs. There were three, desperately similar.

'Girl. 15–16. No older. Monday to Friday 8.30 to 5.30. Thursday and Saturday p.m. and a.m. Take-away food bar. Must be reliable, clean, good with handling money.'

By the time she was called by one of the Employment Officers, two of the jobs had gone, but she left the office with a referal to the third. She turned into the main street of town and met Nancy, an old school acquaintance. On the corner of the crossing, they stopped to chat.

'How's things, Leece?'

'O K. I'm going for a job.'

'Where?'

'Red Rose.'

'That dump.'

'It's a job.'

'Yeah.'

'You working?'

'Got put off last week. He put on a fifteen-year-old.' Nancy shrugged. 'I didn't mind, really. He was a pig. Always trying to feel me up. So I'm on the dole again. See ya.'

'Yeah. See ya.'

They parted. A blister was developing on Lisa's left heel but the Red Rose was just at the end of the next block. Limping slightly, she went in. Piles of grey fish cakes, greasy bursting sausages and withered chicken pieces dried out under the brightly lit counter. A few couples sat at the formica tables, eating or staring into space. Lisa approached a tired-looking woman who was wiping the counter.

'I've come to see about the job. From the Employment Office.'

The woman barely looked at her; she yelled to someone out of sight.

'Con! Someone for the job.' The answer came back in a language Lisa couldn't understand.

'He says not now, love. He's too busy. You come back after 2.30 when it's quieter.'

'O K.' She limped out. The post office clock showed 12.45. She sighed and went to sit in the dusty park. In the shade of the date palms, it was still very hot. She pulled off her shoes and examined her blister. The bubble was just starting to form, to separate itself from the rest of the shiny red skin. She stretched back on the dry grass, looking up at the leaves and clumps of dates. Glaring fragments of sky made her squeeze up her eyes.

She imagined herself going home: 'Mum, guess what?'

'What,' her mother would say tiredly.

'I'm starting a job tomorrow.'

She imagined her mother smiling at her, 'Congrats, love! You hear that, Dad? Lisa's got a job at last.'

But she'd bombed out on that daydream too often for it to have much flavour left. An ant stung her leg and she brushed it away. She felt a tiny runnel of sweat collect itself and trickle between her small breasts. She tried to doze a bit, then she thought she'd go to the library and look through some magazines. But the heat and the blister drained her of energy. She dozed off uncomfortably and was woken by a quarrelling couple.

'Bullshit, you did! You bloody did.'

'Shut up. I never. Bag your bloody head!'

The ugly voices faded and Lisa looked at the post office clock in panic. She whistled with relief when she saw it was only 2.15. She slipped her shoes on again and brushed her legs free of grass and gravel. She picked up her bag and ran a comb through her hair and left the park, stealing a small red rose for good luck. Back down the street she went, favouring her sore heel, and into the Red Rose. Two faces now regarded her over the counter; the tired-looking woman and a skinny girl.

The woman frowned.

'You're too late, love. Con started her.'

Lisa couldn't speak for a moment. She tried to control the tremor in her voice.

'But you told me 2.30! You said come back after 2.30! It's not even twenty-five past!' Tears embarrassed her and she fought them.

The woman shrugged, but she wasn't entirely unsympathetic.

'Look, love. How was we to know yous'd come back? Lots of them don't. Anyway, I'm sure I said two o'clock. Yes. I did.'

Lisa shook her head savagely and turned away out of the steaming shop. She threw the rose to the ground and took off her shoes to limp home.

The house was empty and hot. She went to her room, threw her shoes at the wardrobe and threw herself on to the unmade bed. Her face ached from the unshed tears. Once, she'd sworn to herself she'd never, never work in a place like that. Nancy had described to her what it was like; stinking hot, the heat from the hot food bar in front and the boiling fat behind, the grease, the constant spatter burns, the aching feet and the dreadfulness of Thursday that seemed to go on for ever. But now she couldn't even get a job in the filthy Red Rose.

'Look, honey,' the Employment Officer had told her not unkindly, 'we've got a thousand girls like you on the books.' This had been earlier in the year when she'd still had hopes of a junior office position. 'Girls,' he continued, 'who can type a little bit. What's your speed, by the way?'

'About twenty-five, but I'm practising all the time.'

'Twenty-five,' he murmured, and wrote it on her job card. 'See?' He looked up at her. 'We've probably got two hundred girls who can type at twenty-five, and another hundred or so who can do thirty. They can't get jobs, either. Now, maybe, if you typed fifty—'

But Lisa knew it wouldn't matter if she could do eighty.

'You're young,' he went on. 'That's in your favour. They don't like having to pay more than they have to for people without experience. You can't blame them. Maybe a training job will come up. You've been off work long enough to qualify for an employer subsidy.'

A subsidized job did come in three weeks later. Lisa went to the interview full of hope. She remembered to smile, to look the employer in the eyes, to stress her willingness to work.

Then she discovered ten girls had been interviewed.

'We'll let you know Friday,' the junior accountant who'd seen her said. 'I'll ring you on Friday morning.'

Lisa stayed home all Friday waiting for the phone to ring. At three o'clock, and feeling terribly guilty, she phoned the firm.

'I'm sorry,' answered the new receptionist. 'That position

20

was filled on Wednesday.' Her smugness came over the wires.

'Bev Hennessy asked if you could babysit her kids of an afternoon.' Mrs Brand was packing groceries away in the cupboards. Lisa went to her mother's aid. 'She can't spare much,' her mother continued, 'but she'll pay you a little something.'

Lisa thought. The kids were nice, she knew them a little already.

'Yes. I'll do that. At least it's something, isn't it?'

Her mother smiled at her and brushed hair back from her face. 'She had a woman minding them but she can't do it any more. She has to be home when her kids come from school. Bev'd be wanting you from about four to six till she gets home from work. She's offering three dollars an hour.'

Six dollars a day. Could be worse. I wonder, Lisa was thinking, how that will muck up my dole payments? And I can still look for a proper job during the day. She felt hopeful again. Her mother straightened up from stooping to put a bag of potatoes under the sink cupboard.

'I don't know why Bev Hennessy bothers to work at all. She has to pay the day lady fifty dollars a week. But she reckons she couldn't manage on the Supporting Mothers' allowance. I wouldn't work for what she clears, watching barbecue sauce go into bottles all day. I asked her if there was anything at the factory for you, but she says they're retrenching.'

Thank God, Lisa thought silently.

'When do I start the babysitting?'

'Monday. And clean your room up, will you? It's a pigsty. I couldn't even open the door of it yesterday.'

Good, thought Lisa. I don't want you poking around in my room. That's my space. But as she looked at her mother struggling to cut a pumpkin she felt ashamed. Mum walked in the door every night at 6.15 from work, unpacked the shopping she'd carted half a mile from the bus stop and put on an apron to start getting dinner for the family. She said she didn't mind, said it didn't worry her at all. Lisa often wondered how many years have to pass before you don't mind any more. Tomorrow, she thought with a sudden rush of love for her mother, I'll surprise her. I'll have dinner all ready when she gets home.

'You could have put the washing on today. All day and nothing to do.'

'I didn't know you wanted it done. You should've told me.'

'I shouldn't have to.'

Lisa shrugged angrily. ESP now! She went back to her room. It was so messy it depressed her to the point of immobility. She sank on to her bean bag. She'd wanted to tell her mother about the disappointment of today. But Mum would be sure to think it was her fault somehow. Maybe it had been. Maybe the woman *had* said two o'clock. And her dad—well, there was no point in talking to him. There hadn't been for years. Years of silence between them. And they'd once been such good mates, had such fun and silly games together. That must have been her fault, too.

There must be something terribly wrong with her, she thought. She lay back on the bean bag. No, Mrs Hennessy must think I'm all right, she told herself. She wouldn't ask anyone to mind the kids if she thought they were hopeless. That brightened her a bit and she thought she might even make a start on cleaning out her room. She went to her dressing table. It was covered in junk; make-up, odd bits of jewellery, a brush that badly needed cleaning, dolly magazines that she read for help, and a wilted flower in a bud vase. Where to start?

She opened the top drawer and pulled out a shell-covered box. She looked at the beautiful stick-pin inside, the fairy figure of silver and enamel that Leila had thieved for her. Leila had loved her. Lisa had never had such a precious gift before, even if it had been stolen. She put the box back in the drawer and made a start on the cluttered surface of her dressing table.

As she worked, she thought about the babysitting job

again. It was something to do; she'd sort of feel employed. It was lousy money for minding three kids, a dollar an hour per kid, but it was a start, and she liked the kids. There were twin boys and there was the baby, Charmaine, an absolute delight. Round-faced, and with fat little hands that made you want to kiss the little bracelet all babies have between wrist and hand, a dear little crease that fades as they stop being babies and start being children. One day, she thought, I'll have a beautiful baby of my own, just like Charmaine, and I can hug her and kiss her and she'll love me to pieces. She made her bed in better spirits than she'd felt for weeks.

'But then you're not really available for full-time work, are you?' The Employment Officer was frowning.

'It's only from four to six.'

'Miss Brand, be reasonable. What sales job do you know of that ends at four o'clock?'

She was, of course, quite right. Lisa considered. 'Maybe I could start an hour earlier or something. Or work through lunch time to make up. Mrs Hennessy really needs me and they're good kids,' she added uselessly.

The Employment Officer picked up her pen. She wasn't a hard woman. 'I could change your card,' she offered. 'Put you down as looking for factory work.'

'But even then, even if I got off at four, I'd still need time to get there.' She was feeling panicky and trapped.

'It's the best I can do, I'm afraid. To get the Unemploy-ment Benefit, you must be available for full-time work. That's the law. I'm not doing this to be difficult.' The officer smiled sympathetically. 'There isn't any factory work, any-way. So I think you'd be OK. But say, just say, a factory job did come in, you could stop the babysitting then, couldn't you? You'd be getting good money.'

'I suppose so.' The Employment Officer gave Lisa an inquiring look.

'Yes,' Lisa said firmly. 'Yes, I would.'

'Good. That's settled then.' The woman crossed out the coding and description of sales work on Lisa's card and

wrote in 'Factory Hand' just as someone had earlier crossed
out 'Office Assistant' and written in 'Sales Work'.

'There's good money in factory work,' the Employment
Officer said. 'Especially for youngsters.'

'Yes. I suppose so.'

'O K. Off you go then. We'll be in touch if anything comes
in, and make sure you check the boards every day.'

Lisa almost ran from the office. She knew the woman
wasn't trying to be hard on her. But what does she know
about my life, she asked herself? Sitting there in her comfortable chair in her tailored suit with expensive gold chains
glittering and a good salary?

'The more of us there are,' her friend Dragon had once
said bitterly, 'the safer their jobs get. They don't care. Why
should they? We're their security. We're their bread and
butter if we can't find work.' Sometimes the people in the
Unemployment Office as the kids called it, were real nice.
Other times they made you feel like shit. Sometimes, they'd
look you up and down as if you weren't properly human.
There was one bloke there, Dragon said, that you must
always avoid. 'If he calls your name out, Leece, pretend to
faint or something. He's real mean. I don't know why, Leece,
but you sort of get the feeling he's punishing you. As if you're
doing something real wrong by not being able to get work.
It's all right for him, I told him. He's laughing. He got real
cranky then and made me go for every job on the board in my
age group. I knew I'd be no good for any of them. Right out at
Silverwater they were, too. Most times, I was told at the gate
not to bother. I was too small. D'you think I don't know that?
I don't need to be told all the same. Shit.'

Brenny, Jason and Charmaine were squashed together in
the bath. Lisa had lured them there with promises of bubbles.
White foam from the laundry powder coated six knees, four
bony, two plump as buns; brown atolls in a sea of glistening
white. Brenny was blowing big wobbly bubbles through his
hands and Lisa sat on the lid of the toilet seat, watching.

'Oh, Sharmers! You can't eat them!'

'Look, Leece! She's eating bubbles, but she can't.'

Jason laughed at Charmaine's bewildered face. Then Brenny spoke to her in his serious voice. 'Look, Sharms. They're bubbles, see? If you touch them, they go pop.'

'Pop,' Charmaine said with pleasure. She poked a bubble. For a second her soapy finger penetrated the film, then the bubble vanished. 'Pop!' she squealed.

Lisa didn't insist that they washed themselves. Already the skin of their hands was ridged with immersion.

'You'd all better get under the shower and rinse yourselves off a bit.'

'Can't we stay in a bit longer?'

'Please?' echoed Jason. 'A bit longer?'

'No. Come on. Out you get. Your mum'll be home soon and we'll all be in strife if you're not in your jamas.'

She stood up to get the baby out.

'Oh, Sharmers! Don't put it on your head. It'll get in your eyes and hurt you!'

But it was too late. Charmaine yelled and Lisa hauled her out on to her lap, resettling herself on the toilet seat. She wiped the baby's scrunched-up eyes and tried to dry her, while Sharmers squirmed with rage. Brenny and Jason chased each other in and out of the shower recess like mad things.

'Come on, Brenny, Jace. Rinse yourselves off properly. That's enough, you two! Get out and get your towels.'

Charmaine looked balefully at them with red eyes. Lisa slid her to her feet, leaned over and turned the shower off. The boys protested.

'Oh, Leece, I'm still all soapy.'

'Me too, Leece.'

'Too bad. Your mum will be here in a minute and you'd better be ready.'

In their clean pyjamas, their heads gleaming wet and faces shiny, the children ran to the lounge, sweet with freshness. Lisa squeezed Charmaine till she grunted.

'Oh, Sharmers! I could eat you!' Then she laughed at the look of alarm on the baby's round face. Brenny and Jace showed off, just to please her.

25

'Look, Leece! Look at me!'

'Look at me, too, Leece. Look!'

They had pulled their pyjama pants right up under their armpits and were being silly, pretending they couldn't walk properly. She got them to sit down quietly in front of the television. It was still very hot and the vinyl-covered furniture was unpleasant against bare skin.

'Now. Sit like good kids and watch the cartoons.'

There was the sound of a key in the front door, and Mrs Hennessy, loaded with shopping, came in. The children rushed to greet and hug her.

'Hang on a tick,' she laughed. 'Let me put this junk down.' The three children followed her into the kitchen and watched as their mother put shopping away.

'Have you all been very good for Lisa?'

They all nodded, agreeing that they couldn't have been better. Lisa looked at the kitchen clock. It was a quarter past six and she wanted her money and didn't know how to ask for it. Mrs Hennessy picked up her purse and counted out three ten-dollar notes and carefully placed them on the table.

'Thanks, Mrs Hennessy.'

The woman sighed and dropped into a chair. The children, happy that their mother was safely home once more, went back to the cartoons.

'It costs me a fortune to have them minded. Oh, I'm not begrudging you, love. It's little enough for what you do. I just wish there was some other way of doing things. These days the old poem's different: "For women must work and women must weep." You don't know that? Something we learned when I was a girl. In the reign of King Alfred, it seems like today.' She did look tired, thought Lisa, and her pretty face was pale. 'Get us a beer, love, from the fridge. Have one yourself, if you want. Oh, it's so nice to stop for a bit.'

Lisa handed her a beer from the fridge and watched as Mrs Hennessy pulled the lid off.

'No, I won't have one, ta. I'd better be going. I'm meeting some friends.'

'OK. Have a nice time. See you on Monday?'

'Yes. Bye bye.'

Her step was lighter. She patted the money in her pocket.
It wasn't much, but it was good to be earning something.
And it really was a very responsible job, she told herself.
Only very reliable, grown-up girls get to be babysitters.
The world seemed more hopeful now. Despite the drain-
ing heat, she found she was enjoying the scent of roses
and gardenias that grew in the dusty front yards she
passed.

What if Mrs Hennessy told all her friends? 'I've got this
wonderful girl, Lisa, minding the kids. She's so reliable, so
honest. And the kids just love her. Honestly, I don't know
what I'd do without her.' Lisa liked imagining that statement
very much. And all the friends at Mrs Hennessy's factory
would gradually ask her to mind their kids too. She'd be
quite in demand. 'I'm so sorry, Mrs Eldridge,' she imagined
herself saying, 'I really can't look after Nicole. You see, I'm
so busy. I'm absolutely booked up. Perhaps I could
recommend someone else?' She was hugely pleased with this
grown-up sounding conversation.

She imagined herself leading a play group of little kids.
They'd have painting in the morning, the way she'd seen the
kids do at the Ashford Kindergarten in Main Street; all
sitting outside on benches under the gum trees wearing old
shirts back-to-front, like painters' smocks. They'd all wash
their hands and take their bright pictures inside and pin
them on the walls. Then they'd sit quietly on the floor while
Lisa read them a story. One day, she might even be able to
run her own business, like Mrs Ashford. Little chairs and
tables and low toilets and basins, pretty curtains, and see-
saws outside and slippery-dips. And she'd be so kind to the
kids that no one would ever cry or be unhappy there. They'd
sit on the lawn and eat their lunches and Lisa would make
them real orange juice. Perhaps she would find her friend
Leila again and offer her a job as assistant. It would be
wonderful. She and Leila could live together and go out

27

together at the weekends, and years and years later, success-
ful men and women would stop them in the street to say they
never would have been able to do the things they'd done if it
hadn't been for the wonderful start in life they'd had at Lisa
and Leila's pre-school. She laughed with pleasure at the
fantasy, then ducked her head in embarrassment because
she'd just passed a startled-looking man. But she couldn't
help smiling to herself all the way to the Shopping Village.

3

Verity, shoving a shopping trolley around the supermarket, collided with boxes, people and sometimes piles of goods. The trolley, she decided, was distinctly feral and went sideways no matter how hard she pushed it. On every side were piles of sugar and sugary food: jellies, sweet biscuits, sugar instant puddings, caramel, strawberry- and vanilla-flavoured chemicals with sugars, pre-whipped egg-whites already sugared, and packets of cakes in plastic film. In the deep-freezes, plastic-packed fowls, turkeys, ducks and geese lay in frosty ranks. Tan and pink hams, chemically brilliant, claimed to be farm-fresh, or old-fashioned, while outside the trucks delivered them from the factory. Dyed Christmas cakes and puddings ran off production lines in their tens of thousands, each decorated with a sprig of bright nylon holly. Christmas time, and the abattoirs geared up for full-speed slaughtering and the roads were filled with pig trucks, crammed cattle trucks spraying manure, and tightly packed cages of fowls. The trains from the west stank of wool and frightened sheep.

Verity grabbed necessities in a bad temper and stared self-righteously at a fat woman steering a trolley full of sweets, biscuits, chocolate rolls and soft drinks. She was still staring when her trolley collided with another, the basket catching her sharply on a hip bone. She swung to see Tom Bennett wide-eyed and apologetic in front of her.

'Hell, I'm sorry, Mrs Unicombe.'

'Excuse me.' They'd spoken together and tried to disentangle the steel mesh.

'No, it was my fault. I wasn't watching where I was going.'

'And I'm not used to these bloody things.' Bennett indicated his pile of groceries.

'How have you been?' she asked.

'Managing. Just.' He frowned. 'No, bloody hopeless.'

Verity didn't answer. There was something touching about his honesty but it was irritating. Most women managed a job *and* the shopping.

'Well,' she said stupidly, 'I'd best keep going. I've got a lot more to get.'

Tom Bennett made a nervous gesture with his hand, pushing sandy hair back from his forehead. 'Could you meet me for a drink if I survive this? The pub across the road?'

'I should get home.'

'Just the one. I'm pretty busy these days, too.' A good-humoured smile and no trace of self-pity won her.

'Thanks. I'll be over there in a while.'

She pushed her trolley out of the air-conditioned store and into the overwhelming heat of a December day. The black tar of the parking area felt soft under her feet and the stink of automobiles and vaporizing petrol filled her nostrils. She unloaded her packages carelessly, tossing them into the back seat, bumping her head on the swinging car door. A packet of biscuits burst as it fell and spread over the floor and out on to the tar. Across the parking area, a banner proclaimed 'The Mall puts the ALL back into shopping'. She crossed the road, wanting to be home, wishing she hadn't agreed to meet the policeman.

Inside the lounge she waited uneasily, but smiled when Tom Bennett walked in.

'What'll you have?'

'A whisky, thanks.'

He returned shortly and placed the drink carefully in front of her; Verity thought she noticed a tremor in his hand. At the next table, a group of youths idled and laughed too loudly. Verity imagined Bennett was feeling much the same as she was, uneasy and wishing he were somewhere else.

30

'How are the girls?' she asked, to fill the silence.

He shrugged. 'I don't know. I mean, they seem all right, but I wouldn't know. I've never been that close to the kids. You don't see them all that much, hours that I work.'

Verity nodded.

'I've got Mum coming down when they're home—like now. But she's getting on. It's hard on her.' Suddenly he was fierce. 'What sort of woman leaves her own kids?'

The old pang bit deep and Verity excused herself and the faithless wife. 'She might have thought they'd be better off with you.'

He looked up at her from under lowered brows. 'Maybe. But it's bloody hard without her. I don't mean just on me. But the girls, they're of an age when they need a mother.'

For a wild second, Verity thought he was making a proposal. But he continued without looking up, 'I know it hasn't been easy on Pam. It's a cow of a job—police work —for a family. Even when you think you can plan ahead, something comes up. Police work doesn't come in tidy hours.'

'No, I imagine it doesn't.'

'Christ, the times I've come home and found my dinner in the oven looking like an old boot—I couldn't count them. Pam would understand, but after years of it, it's bound to cause problems. And she didn't have much of a life of her own. It's almost impossible for married women to get work out here. She used to be a good bookkeeper, but that was years ago. Now employers don't want to know about her. I encouraged her to take up tennis.' His face darkened again. His mouth that could surprise with that good-natured grimace, was narrowed again with remembered anger and pain.

'Have you tried to contact her?' she asked, feeling a bit like an agony aunt.

'I don't even know where she is.'

'But I thought you said—I mean, the tennis coach—'

31

'Bugger him. I'm not going to him cap in hand to ask the whereabouts of my wife.'

So it would go on, Verity thought, the light of understanding glancing away and rage taking its place, or pain. Around and around the emotions swing, like the figures of a merry-go-round, getting nowhere, just moving in to where another one has leapt only seconds before.

'And the girls. It's terribly hard on them—not knowing. I mean, they know she's gone. But they don't know why. Christ, I don't even know myself. What can I tell them?'

And Verity saw with a shock that he had no one else to confide in; that such was his isolation from the world and its people that he wanted her, a woman he'd spoken with only a few times, to help him with this most ancient and intimate of problems.

'What can I tell them?' he was asking her again.

'What have you said so far?'

'Nothing much. That Pam's not with us at the moment. But that's bloody obvious.'

'Well,' she said cautiously, 'I can say what I might do. It mightn't be right for you.'

'Say it, please.'

'I think I'd sit down with them quietly and explain a bit. Say that things are a bit difficult between you and her at the moment. I think I'd say—hell, I don't know.' She was suddenly irritated. It's your wife, your children, she was thinking.

'It's been hard for her,' Tom Bennett was saying and Verity looked at him.

'Tell them that. They'll understand that. Kids take their mothers so much for granted.'

'But what about the other business?'

'I don't know,' she replied. 'Do it the way you think is best.' She suddenly wanted to be gone.

'I'm sorry, this is none of your business and I shouldn't be bothering you with it.'

'No bother,' she lied automatically and then, as gently as

she could, she told him she'd have to be going and they
parted outside the red-brick pub. The sun hit her lounge-
blinded eyes and sent her blinking to her steamy car.

4

A low brick wall ran around the front of Lisa's place. It faced due west, like the house, and had been a favourite spot of hers once. A mail box, with a tiny tiled roof, sat near the iron gate. Only a few years ago, she used to sit there after school waiting for her father to come home. As soon as she'd seen his stocky figure turn the corner, she'd race to meet him. Then she'd trot beside him, chattering all the way to the house. He'd have his beer, she'd have a glass of milk and a biscuit. Sometimes, on the way inside, he'd look in the letter box, and miraculously, although she'd checked it only hours before, there'd be a sweet inside.

'Well, well, well,' her father would say. 'I wonder who this is for?' And Lisa would laugh, knowing. And sometimes he'd tease her, pocketing the sweet. 'It's in my letter box,' he'd say. 'It must be meant for me.' They had conspiracies together; they shared certain secrets—but not all.

Special girls' secrets she had always shared with Leila down the road. Leila was the youngest of seven; there were five brothers who rushed everywhere and a very elegant older sister. Lisa was a little frightened of the boys, but they hardly noticed her as they rushed to football or cricket or swimming in the summer. When the backyard was empty of the boys, she and Leila would rock on the swings, their shoes scuffing in the dust underfoot. They would talk and talk; of what they would do when they grew up; of how many children they'd have; what their names would be; what their houses would be like.

'Ice-blue and mauve,' said Leila, nearly swooning. And even under the tree, in the heat of summer, ice-blue seemed the most delightful colour in the world. And mauve. That

34

funny word that seemed to slip from the lips, cool and grown-up.

'I saw a room once,' said Lisa, leaning back on the swing, 'and it was all done out in the colours of a Siamese cat, chocolate and cream and some bright blue cushions. And there was a Siamese cat sitting on the carpet and a model in a cream dress with long black goves on. It looked fabulous. I'm going to have something like that.'

Leila looked impressed and Lisa went on, 'It gave me an idea. You could have a sort of animal house, with each room like a different animal. You could have a zebra—' She choked on that word and had to wait to get her breath. Somewhere a terrible pain had started to smoulder and needed to be damped quickly. 'A—a zebra room, or a giraffe room. Or a butterfly room. Or a rosella room.'

'Mmm.' Leila frowned. 'A rosella room might be a bit lairy. All them colours.'

'I reckon it'd be beautiful. And you could have a lamp-shade with all the different colours in it.'

She stood right back as far as she could go with the seat of the swing under her bottom. She kicked herself as hard into the air as she could. The houses and backyards swung around her; trees blurred past and back, past and back, while Leila tried to catch up beside her.

In the hot summer days, the two girls would make the long train trip east to one of the beaches. Beaches, like pop stars, or the length of hems, rose and fell in favour. One year, it would be Bondi. The next year, you wouldn't be seen dead there, and they made the longer trip to one of the northern beaches. During the holidays the trains were full of kids in beach gear, the boys carrying surfboards, the girls transistors. Leila took great pains to avoid paying her fare, it was a point of honour with her. So there would be anxious moments under the seats behind people's legs when an inspector checked the train, or at the turnstiles at Central where they all poured off in noisy, colourful groups.

The first sight of the beach on those glittering summer days would always bring an involuntary smile to Lisa's lips.

The long sweep of white-frilled water, water bluer than the sky, the sand extraordinarily clean despite its use by thousands and thousands of people, the patrolling beach inspectors, the kids playing and shouting, the adults laid out like rows of grilling sausages in the sun. She and Leila would carefully make their way, discarding sandals if the sand were not too hot, until they found a small space; they would spread their towels, slip out of their shorts and tops and oil each other. Leila had the sort of skin that Lisa wished for, a flawless olive, despite her light eyes and tawny hair. Lisa's skin, stubbornly Celtic, tanned only slightly. She didn't dare use her friend's exotic tropical oil, needing to use one, as Leila noted with joking contempt, only for babies. On their flat stomachs, they would look at boys who pretended not to look at them. There were times under the sun with the easterly cooling their oiled bodies and the cries and the crashing of waves in their ears, that Lisa felt entirely at ease with being alive; mind drained, body suspended. Sometimes, forgetting the dignity of their age, they'd swim and play, surfing like seals. For lunch, they'd cross the hot tar road to get fish and chips or a pie with sauce. Then back again for the long afternoon. They'd read each other's stars from magazines, discussing the advice and its implications on their lives. They'd made plans to rent a place overlooking the beach. 'And I'll get a job with Qantas,' announced Leila, 'and travel everywhere for almost free.'

Lisa wondered what she would do. Maybe a teacher, she thought, and teach little kids when they were still nice and not awful from years at school.

'And we'll have our breakfasts in the sunshine on the balcony. And at the weekends, after we've finished decorating and painting and stuff, we'll go out every night. Wherever we like. It'll be great!' Leila laughed with pleasure. 'And we'll never get married—or maybe when we're real old, thirty or something.'

When the shadows on the sand furrows were a particular shade and length, they'd reluctantly gather up their things, wishing they only had to walk over to their beach flat. They'd wait for the bus, endure the sticky train, and rinse their sunburn under Lisa's shower.

'But what do you do all day?' Mrs Brand would ask, genuinely puzzled. 'Don't you get bored just lying on a hot beach all the time?' And they'd smile to each other behind her back. Now those summers, that had seemed endless and you could dream and hope, appeared a lifetime ago to Lisa.

On certain special nights, Leila was allowed to stay overnight at her friend's place. They'd push their two beds together and tie the top sheet to the bedhead, making a tent. Underneath, they would whisper for hours. Leila told her about babies and boys and what you had to do. If it was very hot, they'd take the air mattress outside and sleep on the grass, waking with excitement every few hours as the stars swung overhead. They had a secret meeting place down by the river, a ledge on the bank, overgrown with bracken and blackberry. Once, daring each other, they'd both crept from their beds at night and met each other down there. But it had been frightening and surprisingly cold, and they'd run home shaking and never done that again.

Leila had given her the stick-pin the Christmas before her thirteenth birthday; the lovely winged figure, languorous limbs curled around a water-lily pad made of glowing enamel and silver.

'Oh, Leila,' she'd said with wonder. 'It's beautiful.'

'Yeah.' Leila had entered her tough period. 'I knocked it off, so don't wear it in public.' Lisa had kept the elfin figure in her shell-covered jewel box, never daring to wear it, liking to look at it and touch its smooth, cool surfaces.

The first time she'd truanted from school had been with Leila. They'd stayed in the place by the river, eaten their lunches by ten in the morning, and fidgeted, bored, until it was time to walk home, swinging innocent school cases.

'How was school?'

'OK, Mum,' she replied as she did every day.

'What did you do?'

'Nothing much.' At least it wasn't such a lie.

Around this time, Leila's family discovered that the two oldest brothers, Nathan and Darren, had been driving around in stolen cars. They weren't seen for a while. Leila herself rarely came to school any more, preferring to hang round with a bunch of older kids who had liked to haunt the gates of the school at 3.30 to show off their independence. The two girls didn't swing in Leila's backyard these days, and Leila had taken to wearing a great deal of eye make-up and bleaching her hair. They met for one last time at the secret spot and Leila was crying.

'What's up?' Lisa was concerned and frightened.

'Mum's charging me with Uncontrollable.'

'Why? What did you do?'

'Nothing much. I took off for a couple of days with some friends, that's all.'

'What did you do?'

'Nothing.' Leila's black-rimmed eyes flashed. 'Nothing bad. We just stayed at a fellow's place and then we came back. He's real nice. He's eighteen.'

'Bit old for you.'

'No, I like older men. And he said I was very mature for my age. He reckoned I looked about seventeen.'

Lisa regarded her friend critically. Under the make-up and the bleached, spiky hair, it still looked pretty much like the small tired face of thirteen-year-old Leila.

'But what'll happen to you?'

'Dunno. She mightn't do it, but. She's threatened before and not done it. But, jeez, Leece, she's mad at me.'

Later, as Mrs Brand wiped her hands on her apron, she had said, 'I don't want you to spend any more time with that Leila again. She's bad news. Her and all that family. Those two big boys are in a home.'

'But, Mum, Leila's real nice. She's my best friend.'

Her mother had sniffed. 'She'll drag you into trouble, too. And she looks like a tart. So no more Leila. You've got other friends.'

But Lisa knew that she hadn't. There were other girls she

sometimes talked with at recess, but they weren't like Leila. You could really talk to her, and she never minded explaining dirty jokes to you, and you could tell her about how you were going to have your house done, and you could argue with her about the rosella room.

That Christmas, Lisa's mum had given her a bikini. Lisa thought it was a bit babyish—pink and white—but it was pretty and it would make her light tan seem deeper. She was dying to wear it, dying to show Leila who'd been wearing her older sister's black one for a year now. But first there was Christmas dinner to be got through and Mum's **sister** and her husband to be endured.

In the house it was 42°C, and Mum was cooking a goose, a ham and a leg of pork, baked vegetables and a plum pudding with hard sauce. The heat in the kitchen was nauseating. Sweat trickled down her mother's flushed face and by the time the meats were ready to be carved, her mother's face looked as cooked and glistening as the crackling on the pork. Auntie Merle and Uncle Cass squabbled their way through the heavy meal.

'Don't eat all that crackling! Grace, you shouldn't have given him so much. It's just dripping with fat.'

'I trimmed it,' answered her sister, stung.

'I'm not blaming you, it's just he's so greedy. He's already on blood pressure pills and he won't take them unless I nag him. The doctor's told him—'

'Bloody quack,' interrupted her husband unpleasantly.

'It's for your own good. It doesn't matter to me if you croak tomorrow.'

'A bloke'd be lucky if he did. Get away from your nagging.'

Uncle Cass shoved a huge piece of pork into his mouth. He really was vile, Lisa thought. And Merle. Why did she seem to take some sort of horrid pleasure in getting at him all the time?

'Keep your mouth shut when you eat for goodness' sake!' Merle cried.

Lisa's parents ate in silence. The Christmas martyrdom only happened once a year. Next year, they'd eat at Merle and Cass's place. Lisa found she wasn't hungry. The heat, the heavy food, the quarrelling relatives and her desire to get away to the pool in her new bikini had quite removed her appetite. Her mother noticed.

'What's up, love? Can't you finish it?'

She shook her head. 'It's lovely, Mum, but I just don't feel hungry. Can I try my new swimmers on?'

Her mother smiled indulgently. After all, it was Christmas Day.

'Pass Lisa's plate this way,' winked Uncle Cass. 'Waste not want not, I reckon.' And he started on his second meal while his wife looked on with disgust.

Lisa's bedroom was a little cooler than the rest of the house. She slipped out of her clothes and pulled on her swimmers and looked in the mirror. The top looked very nice. If only I had some boobs, she wished. But she felt pleased with herself as she trotted to the dining-room to show them. She stood a little shyly by the door.

'What do you think, Mum?'

They all turned. Cass wolf-whistled, Merle murmured, her mother was smiling and her father—her father all of a sudden went quite red.

'Go and cover yourself up, girlie!' he bellowed as she fled in bewilderment and shame. That was the day, she often thought later, when things had changed between herself and Dad. Something had happened to make him angry with her that day. Had it been rude of her to leave the table and interrupt Christmas dinner? He seemed to withdraw from her as if he were angry. These days, if ever she sat on the front wall, boredly watching the cars go by, she would check her watch to make sure that as her father turned the corner she'd no longer be there.

Leila hadn't been charged with being Uncontrollable and despite her mother's warning Lisa still saw her friend. But one day the family had just vanished. Lisa had walked down there on the way back from shopping and found that they were gone. The house was locked, with empty windows. She pressed her face against the uncurtained living room window. Nothing there. Just some carpet off-cuts and one old shoe lying in the middle of the dusty floor.

Tears came to her eyes. Her best friend had just gone and hadn't even bothered to say goodbye to her. She stood staring at the discarded, useless shoe. Just thrown aside, she thought, like that old shoe. And then the terror of high school without her friend overpowered her and she sobbed.

'Hey!'

Lisa jumped. She wiped her eyes and turned. A red-haired woman was leaning over the fence.

'If you're looking for the Goddards, they've shot through. Left last night. Owed six weeks' rent, I heard.' The woman looked at her more closely. 'You're the little lass that was friends with Leila?' Lisa nodded, unable to speak.

The woman spoke more gently. 'No one knows where they've gone. And there'd be plenty of people interested, I can tell you. My hubby for one. He done two weeks' work for that Goddard and never got paid. Offsiding. You tell me if you ever hear from them, won't you?'

But Lisa had only stared at her and then turned and gone hopelessly home.

She had thrown herself on her bed. Both her parents were at work and the last two weeks of the holidays looked ahead with no one to talk to, nothing to do. When she heard her mother come home, she realized she must have been lying there, empty, for hours. 'Where's the shopping?' her mother called down the corridor. Lisa panicked. The shopping? What shopping? Oh, hell. She'd left the bag of groceries at Leila's place, lying on the ground near the window. Slowly she got up to face the music.

'I—um—lost it.'

'Lost what?' Her mother swung round. 'What did you say?'

'I left it somewhere.' She didn't dare say where. She was in enough strife already.

'How did you manage to do that? Where on earth did you leave it?'

'I don't know,' she lied. 'I'll go back and look for it. See if I

41

can find it.' But her mother wasn't listening. She just went on and on at her, until Lisa felt she wanted to scream. She rushed out of the house with her mother's words scrambling in her head, '. . . stupid . . . hanging round all day . . . nothing to do all day except please yourself . . . might have some consideration . . . hopeless . . . in for a shock . . .' Down the street she ran, back to Leila's to find that the bag of shopping no longer lay under the window. She glanced at the red-haired woman's house but slowly walked away knowing she could never bring herself to knock on that door.

Later, she went back to her bed and lay there again. The world was a rotten place, where fathers started to hate you, best friends just left without a word and even your mother thought you were stupid and worthless. She closed her eyes and tears ran into her ears, welled there and then rolled down her neck. 'I wish I was dead,' she had whispered to herself. 'I just wish I was dead.'

Lisa had woken later that night to nightmare. She lay shuddering with dry dream-sobs as the images receded, a dying zebra being eaten by lions, Leila and her mother laughing at the sight, their faces contorted like demons'. It's just a game, they jeered at her, and the more she begged them not to, the more they laughed.

The Christmas of the pink and white bikini she'd also received a book, an unusual gift, magnificently illustrated with huge colour plates; the stories of Hans Christian Andersen. In the hot nights, with the heavy book propped up on her knees, she would read in bed, half ashamed that, nearly grown-up as she was, she could so willingly enter the world of fairy tales. She was drawn to that book as if she were under some spell. Tears would fall from her eyes as she read of the little mermaid, swimming through the murk of fantastic sea-lilies, her pale body gleaming, and her hands crossed desperately over her breast to clutch the radiant phial that would give her legs. The perfection of her uplifted jaw and throat in the picture, the delicacy of her limbs and tail, would send a thrill through Lisa. 'How beautiful you are,' she

42

would whisper—and hate to think of the knives at every step.

And the Snow Queen who sat in stately and bitter splendour in her palace of snow, her hands regal on the carved ice of her throne, her spreading hair decked with frozen gems. Lisa read of how Gerda, the faithful sister, saved her brother from the Snow Queen's powers. She had some difficulty with a boy named Kay, but there was no doubt Kay suffered from the ice-shard lodged in his heart. Or rather, didn't suffer. He lost his human emotions, his love, his pity and his joy, remaining in frozen thrall to the icy Queen. Sometimes, Lisa longed to be the Snow Queen, splendid and remote and as untroubled by human feelings as the Alps. And in the hot weather, it would be wonderful to sit on a throne made of ice.

During those nights Leila's colour, ice-blue, made sense to her. Ice-blue would be the colour of the Snow Queen's throne, a mixture of aquamarine and snow. 'Think cool,' she'd read in a magazine. 'Think cool to be cool.' She would lean her head back against the wall, closing her eyes against the picture of the frozen Queen and pretend she was in an immense hall of ice, where chandeliers of ice-diamonds glowed with dim radiance.

She sighed. It didn't work. She was still as hot and her curtains hung limply. The southerly had not arrived.

She would pad to the window and look out. Even the stars looked hot and fiery as if they were not moving through icy blackness, but were burning against a hot black dome, melting. The scent of a gardenia might lift her spirits and she would stare out at the fence and the house next door. If there were no lights on she knew it must be late. She would put the fairy tales away and lie on top of the sheets until she finally went to sleep.

'Yes, Leece. Tell us.' The twins squashed up to her.
'Tell us about the beach house, Leece.'
'Give us a bit of room and I will.'
It was a story the two never seemed to tire of hearing.

43

Sitting together on the vinyl couch, with Sharmers watching the antics of puppets on the telly, Lisa told them.

'One day soon, when I've saved up enough money from what your mum gives me for minding you—' Brenny and Jace liked to look at each other and nod then—'I'll take you to a special place I know. It's down the coast and you have to go in a train. Not the awful ordinary trains, but a country train that goes—'

'I've been to the country when I was little.'

'Me too.'

'And we'll go on the train and when we get there, it's a bit of a walk, but not too far. And the place is right on the cliff and it's lovely and cool. You have to go down a steep path along the cliff and you have to be very careful because you might fall over into the ocean. There's a lovely beach at the bottom of the path and no one goes there, because they don't know about the path. And we'll have a holiday there and we'll swim all day and you can have barbecues if there's not a fire ban on. And we'll stay in the house and keep it real clean because it's my Uncle Doug's place. He's nice and he likes kids a lot. He can catch fish for us and we'll have fish and chips every night.'

'Wow!' shrieked Brenny and dived on to the floor. Jace jumped on top of him and they rolled and pretended to fight until Lisa told them that their mum was coming up the path. The twins ran and opened the door. But their mother wasn't alone. There was a man with her. The twins stopped short, staring.

'Well, Graham,' Mum was saying, 'these are two of them, Brenny and Jace. They're seven. This is Graham. Say hello.' But Brenny didn't want to. Jace looked sideways at him to see how he should behave. He, too, stood silent.

'What's up with youse two? Cat got your tongues?'

'We don't have a cat,' Brenny answered with contempt. Graham laughed, but it wasn't, Brenny thought, a pleasant laugh. Graham looked as if he didn't like him and Jace one little bit although he was pretending to. He was tall and thin with a pointed face and moustache. He looked, thought

Brenny, like a thin rat. The rat man was putting an arm around his mother's waist as they walked into the house. Brenny hurled himself at her, pushing the man's arm away.

'Brenny! Stop that! You're squashing me. Come on, get your slippers on,' Mrs Hennessy laughed.

But anyway, thought Brenny, he'd got that man's arm away and that was the main thing. He went to Lisa and watched her as she put her money in her purse. 'I don't like that man.'

'Ssssh, he'll hear you.' In the kitchen, the man and Mrs Hennessy were laughing together.

'I don't care. I don't like him. He's silly.'

'I hate him!' Jace was reckless, wanting his twin's approval.

'Anyway, I have to go now. Be good kids and I'll see you tomorrow.'

For three days now, the sweltering state had been waiting for the southerly. Heat-drained people, who normally never bothered, watched the weather girl on television. They followed her manicured finger as it pointed to highs and lows, indicating the mass of cool air that was moving too slowly from the Tasman. They shook their heads in disbelief when they heard the top temperatures out west, wondering how on earth you could get any hotter than they already felt. They heard how birds fell dead from the sky near Oodnadatta, and a young woman and her two children perished on the Birdsville track after leaving their car to find help.

Medical people spoke on the radio on how to keep the baby, or the granny, cool. Find the coolest room, they said, often the bathroom or a hallway—watch where the dog lies—and drape damp sheets around the cot; then play a fan on them. Give plenty of cool drinks. At the first sign of heat distress, take the baby to the nearest hospital. The newsreader sounded professionally worried as she described the death of an infant, left for only twenty minutes in the back of a car while his parents did the shopping.

People dragged their mattresses outside and slept under the stars. Families flocked to the beaches at night where they picnicked and splashed in the dark, white-frilled Pacific. As in times of war, the heat united people so that perfect strangers discussed the weather as they sweated on trains and buses. The older ones said they'd never seen anything like it since the heatwave of 1955.

The houses of the western suburbs, where the temperature was another eight degrees hotter than Sydney itself, became stifling hot-boxes. The television and the papers reported how long it took a young man to cook eggs and bacon on the black tar near Penrith. A perfect three-minute egg, said the newsreader, smiling in his air-conditioned office, sunny-side up. The bacon took a little longer and a couple of local dogs couldn't believe their good fortune when the experiment finished.

There was a rush on air-coolers, and the air-conditioning firms, with tantalizing names such as Ice-Berg and Eskimo, boomed. The take-away food bars stocked and restocked their freezers and fridges, cutting down on their orders for hot food. The air-conditioned clubs and pubs were packed. People in the Public Service and other office workers found that they were looking forward to going to work in the mornings, leaving their airless cottages for the cooled towers in the city or suburbs. Cars boiled on the flat, joggers and cyclists collapsed. One of the sentries at Victoria Barracks fell forward flat on his face. Even household cats panted, their tongues moving in and out between their needle teeth. The surf was crowded during the day, but few people lay about on sand too hot to tread. Kids had to wear shoes or thongs in the street.

The cicadas went mad, hatching in the hot nights, climbing trees to break out of their thin pupae, leaving the brown ghosts behind as they took clumsy flight. Kids collected them like swap-cards; five Greengrocers for a Yellow Monday, ten for the valuable Black Prince. They were stabbed on the wing by birds and their song became staccato and intermittent, like morse, until silenced completely. Cats were sick from eating them. Sharmers disassembled one and had eaten most of it before Brenny found her crunching on the wings. Golden-green Christmas beetles rowed about helplessly on their backs until the ants finished them.

Half past six and the sun was burning hot. It was one of those days, thought Lisa, when the heat just gets worse and worse and you think you'll never stop sweating again. She walked down the street, past the huge words of the graffiti that decorated the fence near her house, following her shadow. As she paused at the corner, the evening traffic stalled and snarled around her. She felt the babysitting money in her pocket. It was late shopping night and she was meeting Marika, Shawn and Dragon up the Shopping Village.

It belied its name. Acres of shops selling uselessness; clutter for houses, cars and backyards; fast-food bars, boutiques selling tacky, mean-seamed clothes; veneer particle boards, gummed and stapled, masqueraded as timber with plastic-gilt handles. And the crowds were larger than any village's entire population. The women dragged screaming children, yelling at them over the distorted Christmas carols, amplified so that no escape was possible from the intrusion. During the school holiday periods, and after school hours in term time, the air-conditioned hangars become a crèche where hundreds of children waited for their parents' return from the factories or shops where they worked. Lisa sighed with relief as the doors parted for her and a gust of cold air enveloped her sticky body. Dragon waved to her and smiled. Marika and Shawn, holding hands, drifted over to join the other two.

'Who wants a drink?' Dragon asked. Everyone. He returned with four paper cups and they drank the soft drink sitting on the plastic seats amid a litter of take-away food cartons and butts. Lisa watched the crowds as they milled around the shops, picking things up, turning them over and putting them down. Some of the women remorselessly followed the specials, checking them against cuttings from the local newspaper. For all the crowds and all the handling of

47

goods, there was very little buying going on. It was like a bazaar; everyone looking for the cheapest price.

'I dunno where they get the money these days.' Marika shook her head. 'There's a million of us out of work and I reckon they all live out here.' There was a certain pride in the figure.

'Yeah, Marika,' Dragon's low voice was almost drowned in a chorus of synthetic angels and violins, 'but there's still more of them working. They're the lucky ones. They couldn't give a rat's arse about us.'

'Maybe they will soon.' Marika pointed. 'Look at all them little kids. There won't be any jobs when they grow up.' Lisa thought of Brenny, Jace and Sharmers, darling Sharmers.

'What'll happen to them?' she asked, alarmed.

Marika shrugged. 'Search me.' Then she cuddled up to Shawn. 'But at least they won't be calling me a dole bludger no more.'

'You've got a job?' Lisa couldn't believe it. She was half envious, half pleased. If Marika could do it, so could she. She waited while her friend disentangled herself from Shawn.

'Me and Shawn are gonna have a baby. I'll get the Supporting Mothers. At least I'll be doing something different—and worthwhile.'

'A baby? But, Marika, you just said there wouldn't be any—'

'Things might pick up again, mightn't they?'

'But you're only seventeen.'

Marika laughed, tossing back her curly dark hair. 'Old enough. And I'm going to bring it up well. It'll be the happiest baby in the world.' She glanced at her sheepish young lover.

'It's her idea.' But he was suddenly loyal. 'And I reckon it's a good one. A bloke has to have something to work for.'

His statement rang hollow, drowned out by a surge of electric seraphim and the promise of a red light special in the motor accessories department.

'But a house,' persisted Lisa, 'you'll never get a house of your own.' And she thought again of a rosella room where

48

children would look in wonder at the birds on the walls, the curtains and the shining lamp.

Later, Dragon walked home with her, but she shook him off near her gate. It was still stifling hot and the roads were full of angry people going home. She *must* get a job, she thought. Tomorrow, she'd go into every shop in town. She'd try her hardest. Another year and she'd be seventeen. So many of the jobs said fifteen to sixteen only. She wouldn't go the way Marika had chosen, the idea of motherhood frightened her. And mothers should have proper husbands and houses and both of these seemed unachievable. But a job—she must get a job.

She pushed open the back door to the kitchen. Her mother was standing at the stove with her back turned. She didn't change her attitude as her daughter came in and Lisa suddenly realized that her mother was crying. This was so alarming that Lisa was almost in tears herself as she went to her.

'Mum! What is it? What's wrong?'

'It's your dad.' Mrs Brand wiped her eyes with a corner of her apron. 'He's lost his job. Him and thirty others.'

'But he's always worked there.'

'Not any more he doesn't.'

'Oh, Mum.' She stood helplessly beside her mother, wanting to comfort her, not knowing how. Mrs Brand pushed her hair back from her damp forehead and Lisa saw for the first time how her mother would look as an old woman.

'How am I going to manage? That's what I'd like to know. The house repayments alone—'

Lisa thrust her hands into her pockets. 'Here, Mum, take this. I can give it to you every week.'

But her mother wasn't listening. 'Eighteen years he'd been with Murphy Brothers. It's all he knows. He's a skilled man. He's done the rounds all day and he's not wanted.'

She leaned on the sink and Lisa could see the tension in her stretched forearms. 'Nothing. There's no work. He's nearly fifty.' Then she started serving up and Lisa automatically helped her, setting the table, her mind in turmoil with this new and disturbing blow. As she set the plates down, she fancied the harmless daisy print on the china was a collection of little sneering faces. The knives and forks felt hot and unpleasant to touch. She set out the table mats; squares of plastic with Paris scenes. Her father came in just as they were about to put his dinner in the oven. He'd been drinking and carried a couple of brown paper-wrapped bottles. No one spoke during the meal and the very silence seemed to Lisa to be filled with painful screaming.

Her father drank his beers fiercely, banging the glass on the table. Mrs Brand rose to clear away, but his large hand slammed down on her wrist.

'You sit, Grace! Your bloody daughter can do something for a change.'

'I was going to help.'

'Help? You're no bloody help! If you want to help, get off your bloody arse and get a job.'

Lisa struggled to keep her voice firm.

'I've been trying that for nearly a year now.'

'Are you going to let your bloody mother support you for the rest of your life? I can tell you one thing. You're not getting anything off me any more. I'm finished. Get a bloody job!'

He pushed his chair from the table and lurched out of the room.

'Don't cry, Leece, he's not himself. He's out of his mind with worry.'

'But, Mum, you know I try. You know I've tried so hard.'

'I know, Leece.'

She helped her mother wash up. She hardly knew what she was doing as she wiped dishes and placed knives and forks in their accustomed places. I'll show him, she was thinking. I don't need his rotten money. I'll get a job tomorrow if it kills me. I will.

She woke to the same grim anger and showered very early. It was already hot and the freshness of her newly washed skin faded as she struggled into her clothes. She left the house quietly, passing the graffiti scrawled on the fence, the roses and gardenias of the front yards. The sun was already high and the dogs she passed were conserving themselves in shade. By eleven o'clock Lisa had walked into and out of every shop in the main street. The blister, covered with an elastic patch, stung fiercely with every step. She limped to the park and sat dejected amongst the empty chip cartons. A hot westerly started to rattle the date palms and the shoppers rushed to complete their buying before Saturday closing. In every shop she had been turned away. Some had been irritated with her request, angry because she wasn't a buyer. Others had seemed sympathetic.

'Sorry, love. I've had to put off my girl. I'm running the place myself.'

Or, 'Come back after the New Year. Things might start picking up a bit then.'

Would things ever pick up? she wondered. And even if they did, would it do her any good? She wasn't very pretty. She hadn't done much at school; she wasn't very clever. Her dad was always telling her she was hopeless. She slumped on to a wooden seat and kicked away a mess of paper and congealed chips with her foot. She watched without interest as ants formed into a line and started marching on the chips. They all looked as if they knew what they were doing, and they were only ants. She felt a surge of self-loathing churn her stomach. She was hopeless, inadequate, unlovable, plain. And quite without worth. Just another stupid girl who couldn't get a job, not even in a lousy take-away bar. Would life just continue with things like this? A fortnightly dole cheque, bitter rows with Dad, nowhere to go, nothing to do except hang around the Shopping Village and watch people?

What would become of her, of them all, the tens of thousands of wandering kids with no money and no future? Maybe she could run away to the Cross. She could live in a squat maybe with Dragon and they'd be free. Free to what? she thought bitterly. Free to hang round the Cross all day and be hassled. She sighed. Everything was hopeless.

The westerly stirred again but brought no refreshment, just hot air moving round her sticky body. There was a growl of thunder and she looked to the west. But it wouldn't rain. It was just one of those white-hot days filled with the tension of expected rain but with none of its release. People with hot red faces pushed past. Someone sent the old chips near her feet flying and almost slipped over. What will I do? Lisa was thinking. What can I do?

'Come down to the Village. I'll buy you a drink.'

She looked up. It was Dragon. He put out his hand to take hers and she slowly stood up and they dawdled down to the complex. It was nearly closing time and the movements of the shoppers were frenetic. They pushed their way through the automatic doors against the flow of out-pouring people. Inside, the cold dry air was a relief after the crowded humidity of the streets. Choirs of distorted angels still sang. They made their way to a counter and ordered drinks. Lisa glanced at a youth putting away the caged headlines of the daily newspapers. 'Jobs shrinking!' screamed one such. 'Retrenchments: three thousand a week! Latest figures!' She looked away and sipped her sugary drink, avoiding the crushed ice on its surface.

'You want to go to the pictures tonight?' Dragon pulled a couple of free passes from his pocket. 'I scored these from Shawn.'

'What's on?'

'Dunno. But there's four different ones at the cinema centre.'

'Probably all crap.'

'Yeah, but it's free.'

'I don't think I want to go very much, Dragon.'

'How come, Leece? You never want to do nothing no more.'

'Just don't feel like it, that's all.'

She finished her drink and sat down on a plastic seat, crushing the empty paper cup and throwing it into a nearby bin.

'You know what I'm going to do?'

Dragon looked up with interest, stirred by the enthusiasm of her voice.

'I'm going to go down the coast. Me uncle's got a place down there. I'll bet he'll let me stay with him. I used to stay down there when I was little. It's a real nice place. Old, but. And right near the beach on a cliff. There's bound to be jobs down there because there wouldn't be so many people looking for work.'

Dragon frowned. 'I don't think there'd be much down there, Leece. There's only little towns down there.'

But Lisa wasn't listening.

'It'll be real good. I'll get a job and stay with my Uncle Doug. He's nice, much nicer than my old man. I can have a swim every day—work in a shop and it will be nice and slow and not like here, with everyone rushing round hot and angry all the time. I went into every shop in town today and—nothing.' She looked at him again and her face lifted. 'There's not so many people down there, so there's sure to be more jobs.'

The idea gave her hope. And it would be cool with the sharp breeze off the sea. Cool blue and green; ice-blue. Old dairy country.

They walked to the door. It was no longer automatic; only those leaving were allowed through. The westerly hit her face as they stepped outside. The sun was directly on the tops of their heads, blazing down as they walked home. Lisa thought of the black surf-washed cliffs and the cool white gulls upswept on the wings of the wind. She said goodbye to Dragon as they rounded the corner of the graffiti fence, and tacked homeward, walking slowly in the heat.

5

The Mount Avalon riot took the western suburbs by surprise, but it shouldn't have. For years, kids had been saying there was nothing to do out there, but it hadn't been till recently that they'd started to realize that this was indeed the truth. As the factories either retrenched or closed down altogether and the shops worked with the barest staff possible, there really wasn't anything for them to do. Many of them had older brothers and sisters who had been on the dole since leaving school. There was, it seemed, only the boredom of school to be endured, the boredom of long, hot holidays, and after that, the boredom of the dole.

There were the clubs, large hangars housing wall-to-wall poker machines, but you had to be eighteen and have a few bucks for that particular form of being bored. Or there were the drive-ins where you could watch a few hours of sex or blood or both and have a go yourself in the back seat. Or you could hang around the shopping complex and wait for something to happen.

So when a fight broke out between two schools, excitement and enthusiasm, those two emotions seldom experienced out there, ran as wild as the fires in the mountains to the west. The riot started, appropriately enough in this area filled with single and deserted mothers, where every second house had no male breadwinner, with two girls falling out about a boy. From being a challenge issued girl to girl to fight it out, it quickly spread. School fought school and the three principals were quickly forgotten. From school versus school it widened until it was kids against Them; Them who came in to try and stop it, adults, police, civic leaders.

Verity, driving back from Parramatta, was puzzled by the

54

many police cars. Sirens blaring, they sped past. She arrived home late; the congestion on the western road had reduced traffic to stop-start for many miles. She was relieved Richard wasn't home, she didn't yet want to tell him where she'd been, nor what she'd been doing. She didn't want to lie either. It would be better if he just didn't ask.

She poured herself a whisky and sat at the kitchen table. Later, on the television news, she saw why the police cars had been racing ahead of her. Thousands and thousands of adolescents were running mad and were still out of control. The newsreader's voice had a professionally hysterical edge to it. The film showed children teeming on the streets wielding sticks, throwing rocks. She watched a reporter, his face hectic in the light of a blazing car, as he redundantly described what could be seen all around him. The camera followed a child of ten whose vigour and enthusiasm were unmistakable as he bashed out the windows of a parked car. Around him, dozens of others milled, yelling him on. A few collected in scuffles, but mainly they just milled around, aimless. Well-fed, blank faces, minds touched for the first time with what their power could do. It was, thought Verity, like the mindless fury of a child that can't understand why he is thwarted. At last they had a chance to get back at their tormentors; those who'd dangled the good life of fast cars and jet-about holidays in front of them, and then told them they couldn't have it.

Richard was very late. 'Christ, Vee, I couldn't get home. The roads were sealed off. You've never seen anything like it. Millions of kids running berserk. I was terrified one of them might recognize me. It might have been unpleasant. It wasn't the place for a teacher to be discovered, I don't think. What's breeding out there?'

'Out here,' she corrected him.

'Well, what can we do? We're agents of the state. We're paid to educate them.'

'Oh, Richard, we are not. Not in most cases. You know and I know that we're paid to mind them, to train them in being bored and staying in the same place all day so they can get jobs which will require them to be bored and remain in the same place all day. They've just discovered that the conspiracy is useless because there aren't any jobs for them to be bored in. And rioting is much more interesting than learning the rainfall in the wheat-growing areas of the world. I wouldn't mind a bit of a riot myself at the moment.'

Next day she visited Helen. The two friends sat together with tea and sandwiches.

'Helen, I hate this time of the year.'

'I know it must be hard for you. But you must forgive yourself. You did what you thought was best at the time.'

'Yes. But if I'd been braver. If I'd been more like young girls of today.'

'It's not so much bravery, I don't think. It's the fashion now to bring up your baby yourself. And it's much more respectable than the dole.'

Verity stood and walked to the window. From Helen's pleasant unit she could see the tall eucalyptus outside and hear the cicadas throbbing. The sky looked white-hot. In the east, Sydney was a distant smudge with just a few towers dimly showing through the haze. She sighed. There was no use, only pain, in thinking of her daughter.

'You know, it must have been someone overweight, or someone with sticky-out ears.'

'Who?' Helen laughed. 'What are you talking about?'

'Jumbo.'

'You're still puzzled about that? It'll probably come back to you.'

Verity looked around. The flat was calm and quietly furnished, the walls adorned with children's art. Odd little ornaments testified to years of teaching and the strange gifts that children bestow on favoured teachers.

'I envy you, Helen. Your life is so calm and unfussed. You never have to share things. You can be quiet and unharassed.'

'Oh, yes. Just me and my cat.'

The cat, as cats do, magically appeared and rubbed itself urgently around Helen's legs.

'Sometimes,' Helen continued, raising an eyebrow, 'I envy you. There's always another adult, an adult that cares for you. Oh, I'm not complaining. And anyway, I'm almost unliveable with, I think, I keep odd hours and I like opera turned up very loud. My mother keeps asking me when I'm getting married and I put her off by saying I just haven't found the man I'd turn Richard Strauss down for.'

She paused and looked at her friend. 'You know, I'm frightened of being found out—what I am—where I work.'

Verity was puzzled. 'You're possibly the best teacher I've ever met. What do you mean "found out"?'

Helen sighed. 'I mean,' she said rather brutally, 'that if I were found out, people might think I'd interfere with the little girls.' Her level gaze met Verity's. 'Have I shocked you? Say something.'

'No. You haven't shocked me—well, yes, perhaps you have. But with surprise more than anything else. It just had never occurred to me.'

'Good. Nor should it. It's nothing to do with anyone else.' She stopped. 'No. That's not true. It is something—something that makes me feel different from others. It's nothing I can change. And anyway, no one thinks the Principal is going to interfere with little girls because he's straight.'

'I can hardly imagine old Talbot doing anything like that!' Verity laughed.

Later, when she got home, she found Richard in the kitchen wearing an apron and a hurt, brave expression.

'Tony was at me again.'

'Tell him I'm not coming.'

'Right. I'll tell him you're not coming.'

She pushed her hair back from her face and tried not to become angry. 'Richard. Try and see it from my point. I'm bored witless by those two weeks on the Gold Coast. I simply don't want to spend all that time with people who have no

57

interest in me. I thought I might enrol in a summer school or something. Improve my mind. I could go up there and join you all for Christmas Day.' The last two words, Verity thought, hung in the air until she thought she could almost see them.

'And—' she rushed on, hoping that he wouldn't take much notice but wanting to be frank about it—'I made a few more inquiries today. There's an organization that traces people.'

Richard looked bewildered for a second. 'Traces people?' Then his face hardened. 'No. You're not to. It's crazy.'

'Richard!' She fought to control herself. 'She'll be sixteen on Christmas Day. Sixteen candles.'

Richard's voice was gentle. 'Don't, Vee. Don't hurt yourself like this.' He put his arms around her. 'Come on, I'll pour you a drink. We should be celebrating. Free from the monstrous regiment of children and principals for six glorious weeks.'

Later, they made well-practised love to each other and afterwards Richard lay smoking and staring at the ceiling.

'You blame me, don't you? I don't know why, but you do.'

'For what?'

'For the one you gave away. For the one we never had.'

'No.'

'You do, you know. And it's absolutely unfair. I didn't even know you in those days, and as for the other—well —there's nothing wrong with me.'

'How do you know that?'

'I just do, that's all.'

Verity hesitated, wondering if she should use a secret weapon. 'Did you think I never knew about that? About Maureen and her abortion?'

Richard, though shocked, rallied swiftly.

'Oh, Vee, that was years ago. That was nothing important.'

She rolled over to face him.

'Nothing important?' She looked down on his well-modelled face that at that exact moment she hated like poison. 'Nothing important. You really are stupid. And conceited. And callous. It never occurred to you then, and it looks like it still hasn't—' she laughed bitterly—'that the lovely Maureen was two-timing you?'

She switched off the bedside light, but she was too angry to sleep. Why on earth do we stay together, she was thinking? In this crazy alliance of two people who are used to each other, love each other sometimes, hate each other in flashes, and keep on going together, tied with mind-boggling and intricate interdependencies?

She lay awake. She didn't often like to think, as she was doing now, of the child she had given away. The remorse festered; there could be no resolution. It was like a long, muscular ache, no longer acute as it had once been. Once it had hurt as much as her spilling breasts. Once, on a harmless drive in the country, the sight of new-weaned calves crying for their distant mothers had reduced her to hopeless sobbing. She read avidly of women who mourned dead children, but there was nothing written of her sorrow. Nothing finished, no end. There had been no death, no funeral, nothing of the finality of the earthly grave; the obsequies of priests and mourners; the bitter readjustment to an empty bedroom, empty clothes. The child was alive and growing somewhere apart from her, bearing half her genes, regarding the world with eyes that were Verity's own, speaking with a well-shaped mouth that Verity had given her, fashioned for her over nine months, and finally kissed before they had taken her daughter away.

The perfection of her baby, in spite of the puffy neonate eyelids, the warm damp head, was an added burden to bear. She had read once, with a surge of horror that would never leave her, of a mother in one of the death camps, tortured for days by watching her new-born baby starve to death beside her, herself being bound nearby. It was as if she, too, were being punished for an uncommitted crime. There was no point to her suffering. It did no one any good. And her daughter, she presumed, was alive and well. But for all that, was dead to her. A nightmare death-in-life, she thought.

On her second meeting with Richard, she had blurted out the whole story. 'He was an academic. Quite high up in the History Department. He wanted me to have an abortion, but I wouldn't. He refused to see me again. Said he'd pay for an abortion, but not the life sentence of fatherhood. He was my first lover, and I knew nothing much about contraception. It was a sin, anyway. I left the university. In those days, pregnancy was not really tolerated amongst the students. I mean the women.'

'How did you manage?'

'My mother was very good about it, really, after the initial shock. But she was adamant I give the child up.'

And now almost sixteen years later, she realized that her mother regretted the loss of the grandchild almost as keenly as she did herself. But it was something they could never speak of; it would be too painful. So Christmas was a mockery to her every year, celebrating the birth of a child.

She turned over and put an arm around her husband. He was sleeping deeply. He was a good man, but he couldn't understand this ache of hers. It seemed to anger him. She stroked his long forearm, soft with downy hair, and folded her hand over his and finally slept.

6

At the Shopping Village, the four kids hung around. Dragon had three dollars left, and Marika and Shawn seventeen. Dole day was days away for all of them.

'I could lend you ten, Dragon. If you can give it back as soon as you get your cheque.'

'No, Leece,' said Dragon with Eastern European pride. 'I don't take money off chicks.'

'I'm not a chick. I'm your friend.'

'Nah. I could maybe get on the garbage run. Although they take the big blokes, mostly, same as the meat works. In June I was out there every morning for two weeks, nearly. Six-thirty at the gates. Bloody freezing. They wouldn't even need to put the freezers on, one of the blokes said, it was that cold. But they just take the big blokes. Or the blokes who've done a bit of boning. They don't think us kids need jobs, too. Makes you sick.'

'Yeah.' Shawn's voice was savage. 'I done every bastard of a factory along Castlemaine Road. Every one of the bastards. Got turned away at the gates mostly. Filled out a few forms. Soon as they know you haven't got wheels, you're stuffed. Old Nerd. Remember him? He works on the nightshift at Allen's. They think he's got wheels. Walks three miles there and back. Reckons he's crook as Rookwood because he can't sleep during the day. Still, he reckons a job's a job.'

'I saw Nancy yesterday.' Marika leaned closer to Lisa.

'How is she? She working?'

'You bet. Working at the Cross.'

Lisa understood immediately. Marika went on, 'Reckons she's making heaps. Still, I wouldn't want to do it.' She snuggled into Shawn's side, and Lisa felt cold and alone.

Was that all there was for girls like herself? Motherhood on a pension or whoredom?

'How can she do it? I mean, all those blokes.'

'She's using. She reckons you'd need to be half out of it, some of the things she was telling me.'

Lisa looked at her, shocked inquiry on her face.

'Oh, no,' Marika shook her head. 'I couldn't repeat them. Not even to you.'

Lisa hung her head. 'Nancy was real nice, too.'

'Yeah. Well, she's kind of changed a bit. Her skin looks awful. Looks like orange peel.'

'I could never do that.'

'Nancy probably thought the same thing once.'

'Hey, what are you chicks whispering about?'

'Nothing, Shawnie. Just girls' talk.'

'Well, what are we going to do tonight?'

'What's free?'

They sat glumly. Shoppers milled about them. Children squealed. A thin, bedraggled Santa Claus was moping around ringing a bell.

'Oh, piss off, you bloody fraud!' hissed Shawn as loudly as he dared. 'Bloody Christmas. I hate it. It's a load of crap.'

The four of them dawdled down to the river. Even now, at dusk, the streets were still noisy with cars and filled with the stench of exhaust gases and heated oil. In the west, the mountains stood darkly in front of a dull copper sky. Smears of cloud and smog climbed in striated banks, still and unchanging. The air was hot and the evening breeze, such as it was out here, had not yet unwound itself from the curves of the sluggish river. They skidded down the bank and sat on the knife-edged grass that formed the dry border down to the water. At the river's edge, a collection of debris formed in little oily bays, plastic bags and bottles, empty beer cans, rotting paper. Even a filthy disposable nappy mouldered nearby. Lisa indicated it. 'You'll be needing them soon, Marika.'

Marika looked at the soiled bundle. She sighed. 'Yeah,' was all she replied. The two boys drifted off to share a joint away from the girls. Lisa and Marika leaned back in the grass, scratching their bare arms.

'Remember when you're little,' began Lisa, 'and you think you can do anything? You think you can be anything you want to be—famous and everything?'

Marika nodded. 'I used to want to be an air hostess.'

'Yeah. That too. But I mean—not so much what you were going to *be*—I mean more the way you sort of think about yourself. You don't know when you're little that you can't do any of the things you thought you could.' Lisa laughed shortly. 'I sound pretty mixed up.'

Marika sat up. 'No. I understand you. I never thought I was going to be an unmarried mother at seventeen, or that I'd want to do that. Jeez, Leece, I don't know. Maybe I'm making a big mistake. But I don't want to be just nothing. Having a baby is an important thing to do.'

'Sure. And it's better than being on the dole all your life. Anyway, I'll be able to help you with it. I like kids. I was going to have two girls and two boys. I had a friend once and we used to talk and talk about things like that. We thought we could do anything we wanted. I wonder where she is now?'

'Probably like us. On the dole.' They both laughed, but Lisa grew serious again.

'And I miss being little. I miss the safe way you used to feel and the way you used to know that Mum and Dad loved you, even if you didn't have money or stuff. You didn't sort of notice it then, because you could have fun so easily. Like if we were here and we were little, we'd think it was just Christmas! You never get bored when you're little.' Then something occurred to her. 'Hey. Does your mum know about the baby?' Marika shook her head. 'What do you reckon she'll say?' Marika shrugged. 'My mum'd kill me.'

Marika laughed. 'Everyone reckons that about their mum. But how many times do you see "Mum kills daughter for being pregnant" in the newspapers?'

'Never.'

'Right. She'd get used to it. And anyway, I haven't seen

63

my mum for a few weeks. It's not so bad if you don't live with them. Maybe I'll surprise her. Take the baby round to meet her and say, "Guess what, Mum?"' She threw herself back on the grass, laughing.

But Lisa remained serious. 'And the other funny thing,' she said, 'is that somehow things don't seem real any more. You know they're real, but they don't seem as real as the silly stuff you thought when you were a kid.' Both girls were silent. Lisa was thinking how odd it was that although she knew the truth about her day-to-day life, she didn't really believe that this was all it was ever going to be. Day after day, hopelessly looking for a job that wasn't there, fighting with her parents, hanging round with her mates. It seemed to her that she couldn't remember a time when this hadn't been the way of her days. And yet she couldn't bear to believe it.

'Well,' Marika was saying, 'we can't go back to being kids again. Hell, I'll be a mother myself soon.' And they sat and thought of that while the western sky darkened and a slight breeze moved through the spear grass.

'And you wouldn't want to go back to school again.'

'True,' Marika agreed. 'That was so boring.'

'Bit like the dole.'

'Yeah.'

Lisa slipped back home, hiding herself in her room. She lay on the bed staring as usual at the ceiling. Her nylon curtains with the small mauve flowers on them hung limply at the windows. There must be something I can do with my life, she was thinking. Something important. I could be a missionary. Not with all the Jesus stuff. Just an ordinary person who helps other people. I could help those poor people in those awful countries on the telly where everyone's starving all the time, not just a bit bored like me. Those poor babies with the funny fat stomachs that have nothing in them. I could do something there. But her enthusiasm was short. I don't know nothing, she thought. I don't know anything that could help. I can't even help me, so how could I help anyone else? She rubbed her bare heels on the crumpled bedspread and

64

thought how she hated, hated, *hated* being Lisa. Perhaps there'd be a drought here, too. Australia was always having droughts but not in the cities so much. But one day soon when you turned on the taps, there might be just a clanking sound and a trickle of mud. The people with swimming pools, she was thinking, would have a bit longer. But even they would dry up and then what would happen? What was the point of taking care of children at all? Why did people go on having babies? They should all stop now, Lisa decided, and look after all the babies that were already here. If all the people all over the world who wanted a baby could take one of those African children—but then their mothers would be so sad. Lisa shook her head. Why was the world such a mad place, she wondered, where people were dying of being too fat in some places and starving in others?

She dreamed that night of her kindergarten. Leila, amazingly unchanged and still wearing spiky hair and black eyes, sang songs for the well-behaved and tidy children. There was a beautiful tower for the children to play on, seemingly made of crystal or ice and vanishing into the clouds. There was an aviary of rosellas, and somewhere in the playground small monkeys climbed and swung. One of them had the gift of human speech so Lisa included him in the story-telling group. She went to round up the children from playing on the tower and the sand pit and looked over the kindergarten's fence. She was frightened to see several large lions prowling around the perimeter where the main street should have been. She didn't like the way they seemed to be measuring the height of the fence and resolved to have it made stronger and higher.

7

In the cool house at Woollahra, Verity visited her mother. Her mother's home was large and empty with a huge overgrown garden. Camellias of the sort Verity liked least, red and white striped, grew about the ground floor, keeping the light outside with their massed leaves. Her mother made tea and Verity sat in the lounge looking once more at the familiar walls and furniture. It was a dim, spare room, reminding her of a convent parlour. And no wonder. Both our tastes were formed by that style, I imagine, she thought. Outside, sparrows chirped and flirted in the heat. Inside, there was only the sound of the grandfather clock ticking and her mother clattering in the kitchen. The scene of that terrible day still filled her mind. Here in this room, I think it was in this chair. Her mother sobbing.

'You must give it up. You must. You're only a child yourself. What do you know about bringing up a child alone?' Bitter words. Her mother did indeed know about bringing up a child alone. 'There's a good place at Blackheath run by the nuns. It's clean and not too uncomfortable. Oh God, why did this have to happen?'

Verity remembered her own bitterness of that day. Nineteen and shamed by the cold betrayal of her great love and its predictable and banal outcome, she had sullenly acquiesced.

Now, they sat together and sipped their tea. There was always that feeling between them of a thousand unsaid things, a million unshed tears, a love that had missed its way, but still drifted like a ghost between them, always haunting, always hurting them. Sometimes Verity longed, with a desire that was frightening in its intensity, to hurl herself into her mother's arms and cry, 'Help me! Help me forgive myself. Help me forgive you. Help us forgive each other.' But the thought of the lost child would rise in a bitter mist that turned away the longing and changed it into something hard and angry.

'And how are you, darling? You look a bit—I don't know—not a hundred per cent.'

'Oh, I'm all right. It's the heat, I think. You can't bear to eat.'

'I've made a nice little lunch in your honour. I hope you can eat that. I don't normally bother with lunch when I'm alone.'

Alone. The word was like a knell. What did her mother do all day now? Did she, too, imagine how things might have been, herself and her daughter discussing Perdita's school results, her new perm, whether she was happy, what surprise they'd give her for her special Christmas Day birthday? Perhaps the empty house filled with noisy school friends, rock music too loud? Sheepish boys making phone calls? Did her mother think, too, of these ghosts? She looked at her mother and noticed with a sharp pang the sadness in the eyes, the mouth drawn anxiously.

'You're a dear. Of course I'll enjoy whatever you've made.' Some relief on her mother's face well and truly paid for the lie.

'Bernice was asking after you,' her mother said, as she dished up the quiche. 'She said it's an age since she'd heard from you.'

Verity gestured, remembering to put her fork down. 'Well, you know how it is, Mum, I don't come into Sydney all that often. It's an hour and a half drive.'

'Yes, of course, darling. That's exactly what I explained to her. But she's your only aunt.' As I am your only mother was the silent implication.

'And during term time, I don't really have a great deal of—'

'No, darling. I understand.'

'But now that it's holiday time—'

'Yes, I'm sure you will.'

They ate in silence. Verity chewed the food determinedly. Her stomach didn't want it, it was already churning. They finished the meal. Her mother cleared away, insisting that Verity sit and relax. Relax, she thought to herself with bitterness. Relax in this room. A room filled with tears, reproaches and love of a hopeless and angry sort. Relax. As well make the same suggestion to the man in the electric chair as you fix the straps.

When it was time to go, they stepped together out into the heat. It wasn't as bad here. The breeze from Port Jackson was still freshly sea-tipped.

'I'd better go now, Mum.'

'Yes, dear.'

'Mum, I wonder if we might—'

'What, dear?' There was a tone in her mother's voice that Verity thought sounded like terror. Surely not?

'No. It's nothing. I'll be in touch soon.'

'Yes. Look after yourself.'

'You too.'

As she drove west, she thought sadly of what might have been. And how unfair she was being, too. Hadn't her mother had a rotten life, widowed with a three-year-old? Working as a nurse in schools and hospitals, taking whatever live-in work she could get where an accompanying child was tolerated. Verity's earliest memories without her father in them concerned a huge stone convent, through which she crept on tip-toe so as not to disturb the shadowy nuns. In term time, the school had hummed to the sound of ninety girls going about their business of lessons, music practice, tennis, rostered baths. Some of them were boisterous girls from country properties, others, elegant city girls who could point out the roofs of their homes across the bay. But during the long holidays, when there was nothing much for her mother to do without the students and their sprains and stomach upsets, Verity wandered, bored and restless, through the silence. Over the high walls she often heard the cries of children playing. Her games were silent in the convent garden.

The nuns sometimes gave her pictures of their saints and

these formed the characters for long and involved games. Sometimes, it would be a school game. Several saints would be propped up along a wall, while another saint, chosen for her nun's habit, leaned apart, teaching. Certain saints were sent out of the room for unruly behaviour, to lie behind a stone. Verity's favourite was a little nun saint dressed in the colours that reminded the child of vanilla and caramel, who held a crucifix and a pile of roses in her arms. The other saints liked her to teach them much better than a tall black-clad nun saint who had no eyebrows. She was very stern. One day, when Verity had been playing this game, she was aware of a nun standing behind her.

'Goodness me, child. What are you doing?'

'I see.' She had smiled sternly. 'But these are religious objects, unsuitable for play. Gather them up and put them away.' Verity had done so and had later overheard a discussion of the incident. It made no sense to her. 'And there was Thérèse of Lisieux rousing on John the Baptist, the Infant of Prague, Anthony of Padua, the Blessed Virgin, and her own Foundress!'

She had little to do with the students at first, being so young. But most of them were kind to her when she came their way. The convents had changed, but always Verity felt alien. She knew the others regarded her differently, even when it was time for her to take her place amongst them in the classroom. The boarders were jealous of her, she who had her mother with her all the time. And she hadn't been, Verity remembered, a particularly attractive child. Her hair was unbecomingly twisted into plaits and she had a rather cowed manner.

Her mother had become a convert, sweeping Verity with her until she was utterly pious. She was as diligent with her new religion as she was with her studies. The ranks of martyrs, the powers of angels, were beguiling for a lonely child, but because she hadn't been born into it, it was hard to separate Heaven from Fairyland. Even the blessed Virgin could have taken her place as queen of the other world, with her crown of stars, her flowing hair and the serpent she trod.

The glittering vestments, hand-worked by novices and elderly nuns, were a fascination. The priest recreated the ancient sacrifice; wearing white for the virgins, red for the martyrs, and green, as Verity early decided, for the more boring saints—educators and confessors. She was thrilled to read of hermits who lived up poles in deserts, devoted to the courage of Roman maidens and matrons who faced the lions, and almost in love with St Janarius whose blood mysteriously liquefied every year in Naples. But she never felt quite the same as the real Catholic girls. So she became more scrupulous, twisted her will to ever harder acts of self-control and denial, sleeping on the bare springs of her bed during Lent. The gloomy sadness of Tenebrae affected her deeply; the statues standing like shrouded corpses, the chapel emptied of its deity. In the shadowy darkness of the black-shrouded altar it seemed that the very heart of the convent had stopped beating.

The boarders went home. It was very hard, one of them told Verity, to be depressed by the events of Calvary two thousand years ago when you were going home to your horse or your new baby sister over the Easter weekend. But for Verity, things were very different. There was nothing to do; nowhere to go. Her mother read and knitted, pleased with the break in routine. One thing cheered the child at these times; that there was no competition for her mother's time and attention. But she knew she would always somehow spoil the potential intimacy with whingeing demands, so that her mother would become irritated with her and send her away. At times such as these, Verity would think that her mother cared more for the needs of the boarders than she did for her own lonely daughter. And so she would run little errands around the empty convent, ingratiating herself with several of the nuns.

Her diligence was finally rewarded with a scholarship to university and that's where it all started, she often thought. Nothing in her education, formal and female as it had been, could have proofed her against the predatory male. She could barely remember what the senior lecturer looked like.

Had he even been intelligent? She had thought so then. But at nineteen, one's judgement of such things is very shaky. That a lecturer could have been interested in her had seemed nothing short of a miracle.

She continued the slow drive west. The roads were already, or still, congested. One day, she thought, the traffic will just stop—clunk, like a huge seized-up engine, because the last possible car has just been squeezed on to the last remaining space of road. The humidity was sickening; the road shimmered in the heat and the filthy bunting of the used-car lots hung limp as if about to melt and drip on to the tar. She arched her back to unstick herself from the car seat. Mobs of kids wandered about the milling shopping centres. In one suburb, Father Christmas, pathetically thin and bedraggled, rang a bell without enthusiasm. Cynical children jeered at his progress. And I wonder where she is, Verity thought. Right this minute, I wonder where she is and what she's doing. Be happy, my darling one, she prayed. Be happy and safe and well.

8

'Here, Shawnie. Read me stars.' Marika poked her young lover's elbow. But Shawn was reading something else.

'Hang on, Mar.'

'No, go on. Read them.'

'Oh, jeez. What are you?'

'What do you mean, what am I? Don't you even know that? You're bloody hopeless. Libra, that's what I am. Look. There.'

Shawn started to read in the constrained voice of the unbeliever. 'Be sure you know all the facts,' he chanted, 'before you rush in and do something you will come to regret later.' He raised his eyes to hers. 'Jeez, Mar, this sounds true.' Even Marika looked subdued. 'Well, it's too late now.' She twined her arm around him and nestled into his neck. He looked embarrassed and Lisa and Dragon turned away from them. The shocked exclamation from Marika swung them round again.

'Listen! Oh, this is awful. Listen to this! "Wounded 'roos skinned alive,"' she read. '"Wounded 'roos are often skinned alive, according to certain shooters. 'Why waste a bullet in the head when they're already done for,' asked an anonymous shooter yesterday. 'They're gonna die anyway,' he said, 'especially without their skins.'"' Marika raised stricken eyes from the paper.

'Mongrels,' muttered Dragon.

Lisa walked home past the huge letters of the graffiti fence. In the last few days she had willed herself to make out certain of the words. They were far too big to read up close. The lettering had been fashioned to be seen by people in cars on the other side of the street, not for pedestrians walking just a touch away. Two huge *F*s stood out; she wondered for a few days if it was just an obscenity. But then she made out the word 'suffering'. And as she walked home in the heat, so hot that even the flies were quiescent, she struggled with the giant letters until she could discern the word 'fire'. She had made a rule with herself that she would not go to the other side of the street to read it; she had to decipher it this way, in bits and pieces. Now, she was thinking, she had the kangaroo to hurt her. Not just the poor zebra.

Her heel bit with every step as she went into the house. Funny, she thought, when you have bad pain in the head, you hardly notice pain in the foot. It was slightly less hot inside and she walked into the kitchen before she had a chance to see that her father was sitting there.

'Where've you been? Out having a good time on the dole?' Lisa didn't answer him. Normally—but she knew how things were not normal nor ever would be again—he would be at the club, or fiddling in the garden with the hose.

He roared at her, 'I can't even get the dole! Worked hard all me bloody life. Paid me taxes to the bloody silver-tail government, fought for them in lousy Korea. Now they won't help me. I went to your bloody dole office yesterday and a kid of twenty looked down his nose at me. Tells me your mother has to support me. Your mother. As if I'm a pimp!'

Lisa thought of a painting she'd seen of a baited bear dancing on the end of his rope. The bear's eyes had been almost human in their sadness and she could never bear to look at the illustration again.

'Dad, I've got to go now. I told Mrs Hennessy that I'd do this afternoon for her. The kids—'

'Don't you bloody walk away when I'm speaking to you!'

'I thought you'd finished.'

'Too bloody right! I'm finished right enough!'

And so am I, Lisa thought. She ran just in time before the tears came. In her room she started throwing things into a bag as the sobs shook her. I'm getting out. I'm going away. I'll find Nancy. I'll find her somehow. She'll let me stay with her. I don't have to do what she's doing. I'll just get the dole office to transfer me to Kings Cross. I might get a job there, too. Clothes were difficult; they wouldn't fit in. She stopped pushing them, blew her nose and took count. She thought of Brenny, Jace and Sharmers, all waiting for her. Mrs Hennessy relying on her. *Relying* on her. She left the haphazard mess and looked at herself in the mirror. A mess. A big crybaby. Just because everyone else is going berserk doesn't mean I have to. She waited a few minutes till the tears stopped and then went to the bathroom to douse her face under the cold water tap. She patted her face dry, straightened herself and left for the Hennessy house.

'Jeez, Leece, it's hot as hot.' Brenny had trotted out to meet her. 'Mum let us play with the hose.'

'You can play with it again if it's all right with your mum.'

Inside, she found Mrs Hennessy nervously patting down the collar of her blouse. She'd pinned a gardenia to her lapel and the pure white petals spun open like an impeller.

'How do I look, Leece?'

'Great.'

But Mrs Hennessy frowned. 'You don't think I'm a bad mother, do you? I mean, going out like this? But I have to have a bit of time for myself. I love the kids, but I'm only thirty-five, Leece. I need a little bit of fun.' She turned to the window as a car pulled up. Lisa looked to see a red sports car and the man Brenny referred to as Ratman getting out.

'He's not interested in the kids, I know that. But he's interested in me all right.' She arranged her face before opening the door. 'Well, kids, me and Graham are going out to the club for a bit so you all be good kids for Lisa.'

Brenny perjured them all and promised perfection. He stood frowning as his mother folded her legs into the little car and held on to her hair, squealing like a girl as the car pulled away from the kerb. But he soon joined in the fun and they made arches of water with the hose and played 'Here comes the Bride'. They tried to skip with liquid ropes and squealed harder the wetter they got. Lisa forgot her age and her sadness and jumped and sang with them. But then she noticed Sharmers, shivering bravely, hair flat on her skull like a water rat.

'We'd better go inside now and have baths.'

'Baths! But this is better than a bath.'

Just then, the sun winked out behind the mountains and the waiting mosquitoes pounced. They ran inside, slapping and yelling.

Lisa mentally saw the kangaroo skinned alive—the delicate face, sensitive and velvety, so much more convoluted, cleverer than a deer's; the dainty, dark-gloved paws. Her heart raced as she ran with the mother and watched while she threw her joey into covering brush, with the dogs and the men after them both. She remembered that the anguish of the mothers as they mourn a dead joey starts another embryo to take the lost one's place. So now she had another terrible thing to know. Now it joined the other terrible things so that they were roped together like demons on the cliffs of Hell. Thinking of the raw kangaroo caused the other horrors to force their way inside her head. One concerned a film she'd seen years ago of a zebra, felled by lions, who swung its head up sickeningly to watch the great cats as they fed off its belly. Another horror concerned an incident at a place she'd read about called Babi Yar during the Hitler war. And the longer I live, she thought to herself, the more terrible things I will find out.

Mrs Hennessy arrived home much later than she'd said, and Lisa was very pleased to see her. Despite having the television up too loud, she'd done nothing but sit by herself while the zebra, the kangaroo and the poor ditch people who were massacred at Babi Yar ran and screamed around in her head. She walked home quickly, trying to shake the demons from her footsteps. The moon was high and the night air had cooled so that the roses were scenting the street. The westerly was hiding somewhere, lying in wait and resting itself until the sun would draw it out next day like a fire dragon from its cave. She let herself in softly and heard with a start that her parents were still up. She could hear their voices, tired and angry, and see the flicker of the television.

'It's not her fault. You take it out on her.'

'Other kids have jobs, Grace.'

'You're angry because you've lost yours. And you hate to see Leece out of work. I think it's because if she can't get a job at her age, it makes you worry even more about your chances.'

Lisa heard her father jump out of his chair.

'I'm not even fifty yet. I'm a skilled man. Am I finished already? I might as well go and join the derros in Belmore Park! No. It's the young kids are to blame. They won't work. They're the ones dragging the country down. I want to work. I'm not like them.'

She crept past the living room and down the narrow hall to her bedroom. She started to pull clothes out of the drawers and cupboards, not with the anger of last time, but steadily and hopelessly. Before she went to sleep, she wrote a note, carefully making tiny circles for the dots of the i's, 'Dear Mum, I'm going away for a bit to get a job. Please don't worry. I'll ring. I know what I'm doing, Love, Lisa.'

She woke very early, just as piccaninny dawn streaked the dirty clouds over Sydney in the east. She closed the suitcase. Mrs Hennessy's money lay safely in her wallet with the elephants on it. She left the house with a sense of adventure such as she hadn't experienced in a year. Her despair seemed to have gone. She took the train to Central, filled with sleepy sales assistants. Saturday morning, and only half of the city was awake. At Central, she waited for the South Coast train. Uncle Doug would be so pleased to see her. She imagined her arrival. Doug would be down there with his big beach rod. She'd 'cooee' from the cliff top and he'd look up and wave, swiping his free arm from side to side. She'd make a sign that meant the kettle was on and he'd hold up his fist, once, twice, three times or more, to indicate how many bream or flathead he'd caught. Soon they'd be sitting round the kitchen table with the old fashioned oilcloth cover telling each other all their news.

As the train weaved south, worming its way around the outline of the coast, she watched with relief. Everywhere was blueness and coolness. From tangled scrub and the lichen-covered walls of rocky cuttings the train would suddenly turn to reveal a blinding expanse of white beach with the Pacific washing it with blue and foamy surf. The southerly fanned her face, as sparkling and fresh as the white-topped waves that chilled it on its way. She could feel her terrible sadness lifting. Here, there were no skinnings alive. Here there was sea and black cliffs and the iced breeze off the white horses. Here was ice-blue wherever she looked east. The funny old-fashioned towns of the coast amused her; the slow, uncontrived ugliness here, so different from the screeching harshness of her own western suburbs. The train followed the low track round the outline of Australia like a tracing. There were oyster leases in flat inlets. Small, dangerous beaches teased the sea, drawing it up in frothy spurts and geysers.

She walked the couple of miles from the station to Doug's place, swinging her bag from shoulder to shoulder as it became heavier. At the top of the rise near the turn-off to the cottage was the small shop that serviced the widely spread holiday houses and shacks. She opened the door and a small bell on it announced her arrival. The woman behind the counter stared at her a second then smiled with real pleasure.

'Well! What a surprise! Goodness me, Leece, you've grown so much. It must be years since we saw you.'

'Hullo, Mrs McGregor. I've come for the weekend. To stay with Uncle Doug.'

Mrs McGregor frowned. 'But didn't you know? He's not there, love. He went out west about—' she turned away and yelled behind her—'how long do you reckon since Doug went?'

'About two months,' came the answer from the back of the shop.

'Yes. That'd be right, love. About eight or nine weeks ago. Said he'd try and find a bit of farm work or do a bit of rabbitting, you know. A bit of panning. He took Lady with him. I pop up there every week or so. Have a bit of a dust round. Ernest does the mowing. A place starts to look sad if it's left to itself.'

Lisa heard the matter-of-fact chatter in a daze. Uncle Doug not there? What would she do?

'He's not the only one who's gone, either,' Mrs McGregor went on. 'Most of the kids have gone. There's nothing for them here. This used to be a beaut little place. Now it's just a ghost town. I don't know what'll happen when they finally close down the steel works. We'll never be able to get a buyer for this business.'

Lisa interrupted her. 'Mrs McGregor, do you think Uncle Doug'd mind if I stayed there tonight? I'd leave it all clean and everything.'

'I'm sure he wouldn't. He's told me more than once you're his favourite. It'll be good to give the place a bit of an airing. The key's here somewhere.' She found it and passed it to Lisa.

'Mrs McGregor, are there any jobs here?'

The woman shook her head. 'No, love. My Maureen's had to go and live with my sister in Sydney. She did a year at the Tech and everything. She's got a temporary job with a solicitor. It's a worry. You worry about your kids. Darren's just been retrenched. Third-year apprentice and everything. Once, if you had a trade, you were set for life, right as rain, not any more, but.'

'No, I know. My dad's been put off.'

'Oh no! That's awful. Your poor mum must be in a state. She's the breadwinner now.'

'Yes. I suppose she is.' She thought of her mother and for a second longed for her. But if she rang now, she'd only be in strife for creeping out this morning. She bought a loaf of bread, butter and some milk.

'That's all you want, love?'

Lisa nodded. She paid and as she was leaving with her purchases, Mrs McGregor called out after her.

'If you'd like to pop down and have tea with us tonight,

78

you're very welcome. We still aren't used to it being just the two of us. I always cook far too much.'

'Thanks. I might. Bye.'

She trudged up the dirt path. She hadn't realized how much she'd been looking forward to seeing her uncle until she found how saddened she was by his absence.

She let herself in by the back door and looked around. The place was very clean. A few dead blowflies were folded up on the table and she swiped them away. She found the fuse box and turned the electricity on. She put the milk and butter in the fridge and the loaf in the big old-fashioned bread bin with rosellas on it.

She went outside, saving the best till last. Out the back, she stood near the door. She could feel the huge swing of the Pacific through her feet. It surged and crashed under her, shaking the earth and tingling up her spine from the ground on which she stood. From where she was, she could see far out to sea, but not the beach. It lay hidden from her, under the shelf of the steep cliff. There was a faint haze where sky met water, but the line was almost indistinguishable. A toy steamer seemed to hang there, motionless. Above her, gulls wheeled and screamed, hoping for scraps. They soared on thermals and dipped on the wind. The easterly cooled her brow and she moved closer to the edge, fearful of being drawn over by the enormous pull and tug of the sea. There, far below her, was the beach, surrounded by jutting rocks. The surf rolled and crashed, then pulled back, gathering itself up for the next breaker. Against the rocks it flew in great fans, or eddied and frothed until the water was the colour of the Snow Queen's castle, ice-blue or frosty jade. Despite the heat of the day, she shivered, imagining all that immenseness of water and the huge power that swept it backwards and forwards along the coast.

She went back inside and put the kettle on. She was happier here. She made tea and went to sit on the step with her cup. She could still feel the great crash of the sea through her legs and thighs, even on the wooden step. Certain waves, invisible to her where she sat, were so huge that the house

trembled at their collapse. She sipped her tea. This would
be the place to live. Here it was cooler. There was the beach
just down there. She could get a job, maybe even in Mrs
McGregor's shop, and Brenny and Jace and Charmaine
could all come down here and live with her and Uncle Doug.
It wouldn't cost much because Uncle Doug would catch fish
for dinner and Mrs Hennessy would send a bit of money each
week. Not too much. About ten dollars a week each for the
kids. With her wages and Uncle Doug's fish, they'd manage
all right. But then she thought of school. No, that wouldn't
be a problem. It'd be much better for the kids if they went to
school here. It would be a little school, almost like a country
school. Not like the big barracks of glass and cement that the
twins would have to go to in a few years, and where eventual-
ly darling Sharmers would be swallowed up and spat out
again with no job and no hope like herself. And the twins.
What would happen to them? They'd end up lounging round
the Village shopping centre all day with nothing to do and
get into trouble. Maybe start on heavy drugs. She went cold
at the thought.

She finished her tea and changed into her bikini. She made
her way carefully down the track, keeping close to the wall of
the cliff and not looking down to her right where the sea
crashed below on the rocks. Spray drifted on to her skin and
made goose bumps erupt. The air was spangled with tiny
crystals of salt that you could taste if you breathed with your
mouth open. She lay on her towel, the only human being
in the world. Scallops of black, lacy sand looped along
the beach, showing the extremity of the tides' reach; the
edging of coal dust from the dying steelworks. The roar of
water and the shrieks of gulls filled her ears. The breeze
blew stiffly from the sea, cooling the heat of the sun on her
body.

She wished the old Unicorn had answered that letter. The
Unicorn had been so kind to her that day when she'd thought
she'd die of shame. Her own Mum even couldn't have been
nicer. As for Dad—sometimes she found it hard to believe
that she was their kid, they were so different from her.

Different looking too. Uncle Doug used to say she must be a changeling. He was real nice, Uncle Doug. Much nicer than her father. Funny to think they were brothers. He used to visit on those earlier Christmas Days, but hadn't been for some time now.

She thought again of the Unicorn. Why, she wondered, did she not answer my letter? I suppose, she answered herself, she's got other more important things to do. And the Unicorn could get cranky, too. There was no denying that. One particularly hot day she'd lost her temper. She'd roared the homework at them, hardly given them time to write it down; sets of maths, two big huge comprehensions. Then she'd overheard something from the back of the classroom. 'And as well as that,' she'd yelled—but you could see that something had changed, that she wasn't angry any more, just pretending—'everyone has to bring in something about unicorns. Yes. You especially, Byron. You talk about unicorns enough of the time, it's only reasonable that you should know a bit about them. Sometimes, they can get very cranky!' And Miss had lowered her head and glared at them and then she'd started to laugh.

Monday had brought a unicorn field day. Pictures, a song that explained why there weren't any left in the world because the unicorn had missed getting into the Ark, and lots of dull dictionary definitions: 'A fabulous beast, usually depicted as horse-like with a spiral horn projecting from its forehead, often bearded and with the tail of a lion.' Miss had told them that her namesake had been a very rare creature indeed, and could only be captured by one pure in heart. She read then from a book, Lisa remembered, that told of the young girl sitting in the forest and the unicorn shyly trotting up and laying its head in her lap. But the boys in the story had been waiting for just such an occasion and they hacked and speared it where it lay, then wondered bitterly amongst themselves why on earth they had wanted to destroy such a beautiful beast.

'Yes, Miss, why did they?' came from all parts of the classroom.

Miss had shrugged. 'I don't know. Has anyone any suggestions?'

'For its horn? Like elephants?'

'Perhaps.'

'What about to eat it?'

'You can eat meat, not unicorn,' came one boy's disgusted reply.

And they'd talked for some time about the mystery of why the unicorn was destroyed.

'Maybe it was the last one in the world and that's why there aren't any left today.'

'No. You've got to have two to have babies, don't you, Miss?'

'Maybe unicorns didn't have to. They might have been special.'

Lisa stared at the blue sky until her eyes watered. I wonder, she thought to herself, what the Unicorn is doing this very minute? And Leila? Wouldn't it be great if she and Leila could buy a little place near the beach, just a cheap little cottage. They could paint it in bright colours and get swings and slippery-dips. It would be much better than the kindergarten in Main Street. The children would have the fresh sea breeze, they could start a sea-shell collection and they'd never have to pay for sand for the sand pit. They could even have swimming lessons if she and Leila were very careful. And there were no dangerous roads here. It would be a perfect spot for a kindergarten.

She could feel herself starting to burn so she picked up her towel, shook it away from her, and climbed up to the house. A veil of cloud had shadowed the sun and she shivered in the glare. Inside, she made some toast, but when she'd buttered it, she found she had no appetite at all. She took it outside and threw it in pieces to the gulls who fought and screamed for it. She put on the radio and sat in the scruffy little lounge that had one of Uncle Doug's shot-guns still hanging on the wall. She tried to read a magazine but found she couldn't concentrate. In the magazine she found a photograph of a two-year-old child, victim of the Ethiopian famine. It was a terrible thing to see despair in a baby's eyes, Lisa thought. And that could be Sharmers. If the drought spread all over the world and all the money has been spent on the dole payments and the bombs, all the children might look like this. She was trying so hard not to think of the children that it was exhausting her. As the dusk closed round, she thought briefly of walking down to Mrs McGregor's for tea. But that would mean having to talk, and she didn't think she could do that.

Next morning she lay awake thinking, and listening to the surge and crash of the sea. She thought of her mother with irritable tenderness, but the image of her father angered and saddened her. Over the last few years, he'd become more of a judge than a father. She was, she realized, frightened of him. And what would she do if she didn't find work?

At least she had the babysitting, but that wasn't regarded as proper work. Funny, she thought, how minding them and playing with them and making them laugh isn't considered real work. You've got to be a teacher and yelling at them or making them learn stuff about rainfall in the wheatbelt before there's any chance of getting properly paid for it. But then there were good teachers like the Unicorn. She didn't have that special voice that clergymen and teachers used.

She flung her legs out of bed. Outside, the easterly creaked the old house and she padded to the kitchen to make tea. She'd left the lid off the bread bin and there were ants everywhere, deeply embedded in the fabric of the bread. The sight of them destroyed her weak appetite and she had tea sitting on the back step, watching the gulls as they wheeled and fought for the ant bread. Out to sea, a dirty haze threatened from the horizon. But the sun still shone hot and brilliant overhead. She seemed to sit there for hours. She imagined the streets of Sydney reduced to dust and rubble, and Sharmers and the twins, filthy and gaunt, picking through the rubbish with flies clustered in their eyes. Or worse, as in that film about the bomb, she imagined them, horribly disfigured and burnt, crying for help that would never come. She opened her eyes wide and stared out at the blue glare, hoping to dispel the terrible images. Here, she hoped, they could all be safe.

Inside, she found an old writing pad with a faded film star on the front and she sat at the table with a pencil. A terrible idea, so terrible that it blocked out the suffering of the animals and the children and the ditch people being killed at Babi Yar was forming in her mind. She stared a long time out of the salt-smeared glass of the kitchen window. Outside, the world was a blue mist. Nothing seemed real out there. She started to write a letter.

On the train going west again, she thought it got hotter and hotter with every mile. At Parramatta, the heated air scorched her nostrils to breathe it. And it was hotter when she finally stepped off the train in her home station. She lugged her bag over a shoulder and slouched towards home. Despite the frightening idea she'd hinted at in the letter there was still a bit of her that was looking forward to seeing the kids again. Up the last street she went and tried again to trace the graffiti letters into words. But they remained obscure and apart. She turned into the driveway, into the kitchen and nearly stumbled to the floor when her father loomed out of nowhere and hit her hard, very hard across the face.

Hours later she was alone, dry-eyed, in her room. No, she'd told them, she'd just gone away. Just away. She'd been disgusted by their questioning. There hadn't been a man. She hadn't gone with a man. A curious sense of detachment provided relief from their probings. She couldn't be their daughter. They were strangers to her. She just lived with them. Lisa knew she would rather die than let them know where she'd been. They threatened her with the Welfare, with being Uncontrollable, and still she wouldn't tell. If they guessed about the beach house, their shadows would fall across the landscape and it would never be just her place again. Once or twice, she had looked at them and wondered what they would have said if she'd told them.

9

'I don't like it, Vee. I don't like it at all.' Helen handed back the letter.

'And the awful thing is, that I can't answer her. I've lost the first one. Oh, that was harmless enough, I think. But it had the damned address on it and I can't find it.' The two women stood looking at each other. 'It could be here some-where, or I might have chucked it. Or Richard.'

'What've I done now?' came Richard's cheerful voice from the kitchen. Verity went in and showed him the letter. He read it. He shrugged briefly. 'Just a mad adolescent. They're all mad. That's why they pay people like us to take them off their parents' hands all those years. It's got nothing to do with education. Their parents would kill them. We're paid not to.'

'It doesn't worry you?'

'That letter? No. They all get terrible ideas every now and then. Like they mightn't be the most interesting and impor-tant person in the world. Like the world mightn't turn for their special delight. It's a shock to the little buggers. Anyway, who wants a drink? Helen?'

'No thanks, Richard. I'd better get home to the cat. And I've got huge amounts of domestic work before I can start enjoying the holidays.' Verity walked with her friend to the door. 'Come over one night next week and we'll have dinner.'

'I'd love to,' said Verity, kissing her.

She went back inside and started the search. As in every house, there were collecting points for old receipts, cuttings that seemed important once, silly things that couldn't quite be thrown away yet. She rummaged through the fruit bowl that had never once held fruit in it. She became irrationally angry with Richard who could just lounge around like that sucking on a tin of beer and leafing through a newspaper when she was trying so hard to find the first letter. She banged about. Richard looked up, swung his legs off the couch, collected his paper and beer.

'It's that time of the year,' he muttered as he went into the bedroom and shut the door. Verity was enraged. She flew to the door and jerked it open.

'Don't say that! Don't say cruel things like that! You don't know what it's like.' She could feel herself trembling with rage and sorrow as the words surged. 'Every time I read of a fifteen-year-old girl found dead, or raped, or both—every time I read of a collision involving a fifteen-year-old girl—or when I read of unidentified young bodies found thrown away in the bush, I think it might be her. It might be my lost girl. I'll never know. And even if I were to go to the—wherever you go to identify bodies—and even if I looked into her face and it was her, I'd never know. I wouldn't even know.' She covered her face with blind fingers and Richard was beside her, holding her, murmuring. 'You can't know what it's like. It's such suffering that I can't—' But she couldn't continue.

They went out for dinner. It seemed best to get out of the house where the air was still thick with pain and remorse. They ate pasta and drank too much house red. On the way to bed, Verity picked up the letter again: 'Dear Miss,' she read, forming the words carefully as if the very sound and shape of them might give her some clue. 'I was sad when you didn't answer my letter. I really want to hear from you because there isn't anyone else in the world I can talk to now. My dad has been retrenched. I haven't got anyone. I have these terrible ideas and I can't stop thinking about them. Sometimes the ideas seem good but most of the time I am very, very frightened. I need someone to talk to. Please write to me today. I hope you and Mr Unicombe are both very well.'

'How you could forget someone called Jumbo,' said Richard as he went to bed, 'is almost a contradiction in terms.'

Verity lay awake for a long time, unable to sleep, tormented by her loss and an indecent biliousness. She stroked Richard's arm. He was like most men of his time, too inclined to let her do the lioness's share of the domestic work, pay the bills, administrate. But these things weren't of much importance, really. She turned over on her side and tried to sleep. But her thoughts were racing as her mother, her husband and her daughter, as well as Jumbo, chased themselves around her mind. The old anger with her mother swung her stomach over and she fumbled in the darkness to find the sleeping tablets in the bedside table. No, she told herself. Do it cold for once. She punched the pillows up into a shelter and leaned back.

Why this anger? she asked herself. I'm thirty-five years old and I'm angry with my mummy? She thought of her mother in the cool, large house. Did she, too, lie awake like this? Perhaps even now the two of them were awake, spanning the suburbs with angry thoughts of love. The last four words repeated themselves like a mantra and she slowly drifted off to sleep.

In her dream, her mother called her, but Verity couldn't come. 'I'm thirty-five,' she announced, 'and I can't come home.'

'Just for a little while, darling, just for the holidays.'

But Verity stood defiant in the dream-scape. 'No,' she answered her mother, 'in the holidays you don't ever love me.' And in the dream Verity slipped out into the convent garden that was also her own backyard and sat under a tree because her lost daughter might be coming home for the holidays. She woke at dawn, but the actuality of the dream slipped away as she wakened, leaving only its ghost, a sadness that haunted the morning.

I O

Lisa walked up the path to the Hennessy house and noticed Brenny's jet plane stuck nose-first in a ragged rose bush and a plastic man with a parachute entangled nearby. She smiled to herself as she knocked, and jumped as the door was yanked open, leaving her with her fist foolishly up in the air.

'Where the hell do you think you've been?' Bev Hennessy was furious, her pretty face hard and pale. Lisa stared in shocked silence. 'Where were you last night? I needed you. My sister in Canberra's very ill. I was supposed to go last night—and then you don't turn up when I really need you.'

'I didn't know, Mrs Henn—'

'Didn't know? I left a note for you at your mother's.'

'But I still didn't know. I wasn't there.'

Mrs Hennessy looked hard at her and decided she was lying. 'Look, Lisa, you're no good to me or the kids if you're not reliable.' Mrs Hennessy looked as if she might cry. 'You don't know what it's like trying to do the right things by your kids without any help.' Then her face hardened. 'Now, off you go. I've got someone else. I don't want you working for me any more.'

'But it's Monday. I always come on Mondays.'

'Not any more you don't. I'm sorry, Lisa. But it's just not good enough.' Behind the woman, Lisa could hear Sharmers crying, disturbed by the anger in her mother's voice. Then the front door was firmly shut and she was left standing there, staring at the green and red plastic holly wreath that adorned it. She turned and walked away, heart racing, tears of shame and hurt blinding her way. Her eyes could only see as if they were looking through a narrow tube. All around was darkness. She stumbled down the road not even knowing where she was, where she was heading. The hot sunlight seemed to be different, dark somehow, as if eclipsed. Bird songs and the sounds of traffic came from somewhere miles and miles from her ears. A dog barked nearby, his voice oddly muffled. She walked on and on, turning corners, crossing roads, waiting like an automaton at the traffic lights. Her head seemed to be stuffed with some awful hissing material that burned behind her eyes and filled her ears. She didn't know or care where she was going. A car's brakes screamed beside her; she barely flinched.

'Stupid bloody chick! Watch where you're going! What are you trying to do? Get yourself killed?'

She kept going one foot after another, after another. She found herself at Dragon's place. She walked round the back and found him sprawled on the veranda, reading a motor-bike magazine.

He looked up, smiled, then frowned.

'Hey, Leece, what's up?'

She flopped down beside him and shook her head. Then the tears came and she sobbed and sobbed while Dragon awkwardly patted her shoulder and tried not to feel too embarrassed.

'And she's so unfair,' she stammered finally. 'I didn't even know. And I'll miss the kids so much. And they'll miss me.' Instead of her earlier visions of being the most sought-after babysitter in the west, she now imagined Mrs Hennessy to be saying, 'Absolutely hopeless. I had to get rid of her, you know. You couldn't rely on her. And I was never too sure about her honesty, either.'

'Look, Leece,' Dragon was saying, 'I'll bet you could get more babysitting. Maybe Mrs Hennessy will calm down. She's probably real upset about her sister and she's taking it out on you. Why don't you go back in a few days? Or get your mum to write to her and explain why you never got the note?' But Lisa shook her head violently.

'No. I never want to talk to her again. I hate her. I just hate her.'

Dragon poured her a coke and she felt a bit better. 'Dragon,' she said, 'I think there's something terribly wrong with me.'

'What do you mean? You're all right, Leece.'

'No, I mean it. Awful things seem to happen to me all the time. And I have these terrible fears and things in my head all the time.' In a low voice, she told him of the dreadful things that haunted her.

'What can I do, Dragon? What can I do to forget them now that I know?'

'But, Leece, there's lots of dreadful things. There's good things too, you know. Some people are real good and do lots of good for other people—you know, like doctors and stuff that go to the jungles.' His narrow brown eyes looked anxiously at her. 'You could spend all your life worrying about the dreadful things. You'd go mad if that's all you ever thought about.'

'I think it *is* just about all I can think about now. It gets bigger and bigger all the time. Sometimes the ditch people at Babi Yar seem realer to me than you do sitting here beside me. I can see their faces. I can see the way they try and put their poor hands up to stop the bullets and the blades.' She put her own hands over her eyes. 'I can't keep them out of my mind. They live in here. It's their place, now.'

'Leece. Leece.' Bravely, Dragon put an arm around her. 'Leece, they're finished now. They're not hurting any more. No one can hurt them ever again. Not the kangaroo, either. Or the old zebra. They're dead and gone and finished and they don't hurt any more.'

She rocked beside him. 'But I do,' she moaned, 'I do.'

'Leece, they're finished. Try and remember that. They're finished. Dead. They don't hurt any more.'

Finally, she went home and dawdled about. She didn't know where Mum and Dad were, didn't care. She was just relieved they weren't there. She switched on the television and flicked from channel to channel. Men fought, screamed, died. They strangled or made love to women with lacquered hair and made-up eyes. She watched for a while then switched it off. She went to her room. It was very hot. She lay on the bed.

That night she dreamed of the kindergarten again. Brenny, Jace and Sharmers were there. She went to get them down from the tower when she noticed they were missing. A large hole had been torn in the fence and the lions were no longer outside. She screamed with fear, a silent nightmare scream, and ran inside the kindergarten. All the children were inside, white and fearful. She piled furniture against the door and windows and looked out. She could see nothing but the dry lawns and benches of the playground. But she knew without seeing them that the lions were padding about out there.

Next evening, she was hungry with longing to see them. I'll just pop round, she thought. Just to see them, see how they are. Make sure they're happy. She felt again the burn of shame and guilt. It wasn't my fault, she told herself. But somewhere, she could hear a thin, ugly voice saying, Yes, it was. Everything's your fault. You screw everything up. It's all your fault.

Her sense of shame was so strong that it made her creep like a thief to the back lane behind the Hennessy house. She climbed to stand on the fence's support beam and looked over. She could see lights on, but the house was quiet. Carefully, she climbed over and jumped down. She walked up the backyard, turning off the hose that she could hear dripping. In the kitchen she could see the remains of two meals on the table and a mess on the lid of Sharmers's high chair. She went right in and could hear the television blaring. But suddenly, cutting through that noise, came the sound of Sharmers's crystal-smashing yell. She ran into the lounge room and the three of them turned in surprise, then delight. The twins rushed to her, squealing her name while Sharmers almost turned inside out on the floor with excitement. The boys both talked together too fast while Sharmers banged a spoon and a fork on the floor.

'Leece, she's real mean. She's awful.'

'Who?'

'That Thelma. She minds us now and she's real mean.'

'I hate her!' cried Brenny.

'Me too!'

Charmaine crinkled up her eyes and cried formless sounds of disapproval. Lisa sat on the floor with them. 'She made us a real yucky dinner and then she made us eat it. It was meat loaf and she didn't even light the oven. It looked just the same when it came out and she didn't even care.' Brenny frowned as he reported. 'And,' he said, a judge delivering his most formal pronouncement at the last, 'she even smacked Sharmers and Sharmers is only a baby.' Sharmers, reminded of this injustice, scowled and squeezed out a couple of plausible tears. Lisa grabbed her and hugged her till she grunted. 'She's real awful, Leece. I wish you still minded us. And tonight she's gone to the club and she's not even supposed to leave us little kids alone. She said she was just getting milk and that was before *Dr Who*.' Sharmers kicked and struggled and Lisa put her down.

'Will you stay with us, Leece?'

She nodded. There was a lot to do; things to show her, new toys, an almost healed cut, and Jace wobbled a very loose front tooth for her. Brenny told her of his hopes for a dump truck for Christmas. Sharmers rolled on her stomach and grabbed the spoon and fork she'd thrown away before. These were new. 'Fuck!' she kept saying, to the huge delight of Brenny and Jace who shrieked to hear her. Lisa laughed too.

'*Fork*, Sharmers. Spoon and fork.' Sharmers laughed again.

'Fuck!' she squealed and showed the bears on the ends of the cutlery to Lisa. Then she rolled over in an ecstasy of self approval.

'Come on. I think you'd all better get ready for bed.' The twins looked resigned. 'Come on, Sharms, I'll wash your face.' She carried the heavy baby into the bathroom and sat on the closed toilet lid with her. Carefully she wiped the little

93

girl's face with a warm, damp cloth while Charmaine ducked and flinched impatiently. 'Oh, you beautiful, beautiful Sharms,' Lisa whispered.

Charmaine looked up at her then frowned. She poked a gentle finger into a tear on Lisa's cheek. 'Pop?' she asked.

In a while she had them settled, promising to leave the light on. She went to the kitchen and started clearing away. Brenny had been quite right. There was raw meat loaf held together by flour. The potatoes were still uncooked on the stove. She stacked the plates and wiped the red lumps of meat loaf from the table. She sat and watched the clock. It was ten past ten. This was very bad indeed, she was thinking. And Mrs Hennessy preferred this stupid Thelma to her, a woman so hopeless she couldn't even light the oven but was better than she was. Anything could have happened. What if she'd turned the oven on and not lit the gas? The kids might all be dead. Or what if they'd played with the matches, or Sharmers had slipped in the bath? She looked around the vinyl and veneers of the kitchen, seeing instead a death-trap of possibilities—insecticides, ammonia, gas, fire, electricity. That stupid woman was still at the club, time enough for each of the children to have died several times. Lisa sat quite still at the table and thought and thought.

Later, she quietly left the sleeping household. They were safe enough now, sleeping, she hoped. That woman would have to be back soon. Outside the night was still very hot. A dry, white moon whitewashed the letters of the graffiti fence and caused black shadows to grow in the gardens. Lisa wondered if the shadows hid lurking dangers; she shuddered at the thought of some one or some thing huddling in the blackness under the children's window; a shapeless, slimy thing that would insinuate a tentacle over the window-sill and flow itself over. She hurried her pace. The gardenias and roses of the familiar street seemed different, blacker and swollen with menace. She broke into a trot, then a run, careering at full speed around the corner. She crept into the house, trying to steady her breath. A light went on as soon as she'd stepped into the kitchen. Her mother stood blinking in

94

her dressing-gown. Her face showed anger, concern and something else that gave Lisa heart.

'Oh, Mum,' she cried, 'don't be angry. I've been at the Hennessys'.' She was about to continue, to explain what had happened to Thelma, but she stopped. She couldn't tell her mother that. She couldn't expose yet another of her own defeats.

'It's very late.'

'Yes, but Mrs Hennessy had to go away suddenly—'

'Oh, heavens,' her mother gestured, 'I forgot to give you that message last week. From Bev. With everything going on and your father.' She shook her head. 'I'm sorry, love. I just forgot.' Here was hope after all. Perhaps her mother could speak to Mrs Hennessy, explain that she'd forgotten to pass on the message to her daughter. Perhaps everything wasn't as it seemed.

'Mum, can I talk to you for a minute?'

But her mother was turning. 'It's very late, love. Can't it wait till morning?'

Lisa nodded. Of course it could. It could wait for ever. There was no point. But a surge of desperate hope broke through. 'Please, Mum, it's urgent. I have to talk to you about—about everything. I feel terrible.'

'You're not sick, are you?'

'No. It's not like that.'

'Leece, I'm very tired. Look, it's almost one o'clock. You tell me anything that's on your mind in the morning. I'll have a clear head then. I can hardly think straight with this migraine.' She kissed her daughter and went back to bed.

Lisa walked slowly to her room and switched on the light. Then she threw herself on the bed. But a little voice of hope whispered, In the morning, and she repeated the phrase to herself until it fell apart into nonsense sounds. But I *can* tell Mum, she thought. She does love me. Sometimes she's cranky, but that's only when I do hopeless, stupid things that irritate her. Tomorrow I *will* tell her.

She lay on her back, staring at the ceiling and slowly the dreadfulness began to grow again, pushing out the little hope with it. It swelled and swelled until her head was filled with its mockery. Tell your Mum what? it sneered. About the animals? About the kindergarten and the lions? About the terrible, good idea? How could you even start? Lisa tried not to listen to the sneerer. She knew that the animals, the children and the dream kindergarten were all somehow part of the same thing. But what was the thing? It was fear, and it was hate, and it was a horrid aching thing that filled up a void in her. It was hatred for the cruelty of beast to beast, hate for the torturers of the ditch people. And the fear. Even the dream kindergarten—once a pleasant daydream that had comforted her, made her laugh out loud that day in the street—was now menacing because the lions had found it. And Brenny, Jace and Sharmers were somehow in all this and were in great danger from the lions. But she could save them all, and herself with them.

She rolled over on to her side and stared at the wall. Normally, she hated to lie like that, with her back exposed to anything that might come through the doorway. She stared at the wall. A tiny crack, no bigger than a spider's web, ran across the wall just at eye level. She traced it with a forefinger, finding its tiny roughness until she felt where it ended. She was glad that it stopped. There was something very frightening, she thought, about the idea of a crack that never finished. A crack was bad enough, because it might widen and something might be able to get in through it. But a crack that never finished, that went on and on around the world's circumference, was terrifying. It could split the globe right open one day. She closed her eyes tightly. And there is a crack in me, she thought, behind eyes that ached and trembled with the force of their closing. A crack that is getting wider and one that might just let a lion's paw through, then its fringed foreleg, then—she shivered. How could she explain this, sneered the voice? Mum would think she was mad. Maybe I am mad, she thought. No. Mad people do mad things. They're crazy. They laugh when other people cry. You could tell a mad person by the way they acted. She, on the other hand, felt she was afflicted with some awesome sanity, that she alone could see certain things clearly.

Why couldn't everyone else? Why do they seem not to know about the dreadful things and seem to be happy? Round and round her thoughts chased each other like rats. Sometimes she thought she was able to corner one and kill it, but just a second later she would find it, still dragging itself around the circle.

Without removing her clothes, she pulled the sheet over herself. She lay quite still, staring at the central light. Let me be the Snow Queen, she prayed. Let me be cold and untouched by pain. She stretched out, imagining herself in the palace of snow and ice. The rats stopped leaping about her head. She thought of the children. She imagined them lying asleep, safe and peaceful. She imagined herself cuddling an oddly acquiescent Sharmers. But they weren't safe. They were sleeping in that empty house where anything could get in.

She threw back the sheet and swung out of bed. She gathered up a few clothes and slung them in her carry bag. She took her new bikini from its drawer and thought briefly and sadly of another pink and white one. She stood in her doorway and looked around her room. Her unmade bed, the square dressing table with its pretty mirror that Mum had given her, the cupboard where all her clothes hung, her bedside table with its drawer that always stuck. She went over and tugged it open. Inside was a little shell-covered box and there, sitting on the top of her other bits and pieces, lay Leila's stick-pin: the fairy figure with its enamelled wings and floating hair. She picked it up and shoved it into her bag, then switched off the light and crept out of the house.

The Hennessy house looked just as she'd left it, except now it was piccaninny dawn and a darker grey separated the mountains from the sky. She tiptoed up to the lounge room window. The television was showing the grainy static of a shut-down channel; the room was empty. She let herself in, sensing already that the children were still alone in the house. She checked their rooms. They were safely sleeping.

Oh, I wish, thought Lisa fiercely, that Mrs Hennessy would come home, right away now, and see what she's replaced me with. And I wish she could see that I'm here and that I care so much. I'll let them sleep a little longer, she thought, and then let our holiday begin.

She dumped her bag, lay on the vinyl couch and watched stars fade in the window. Later, she switched the television back on. She experienced the awful fear that the two-dimensional creatures jumping and gawking on the screen were more real than she was. She took one of Brenny's pencils from the floor and found some paper. She had a pre-stamped envelope in her carry bag. She looked at the hand that was holding the pencil. It looked real enough, firm and strong. 'I'll give them a wonderful Christmas party,' she wrote, 'and then—' The pencil slid across the paper. She tried to explain about the lions, the kindergarten and the terrible danger. Their mother had left them—deserted them, really—and got a stupid drunk to mind them. She couldn't really love them if she'd done that. And someone who smacked Sharmers. If only, thought Lisa, it was all over and I'd done it safely. Removed them from all danger. And they would never have to know about all the terrible things. They must never find out. She felt she was a person in a play who alone knew the dialogue and events of all the other characters. If I keep it from them, she thought, they'll never have to know and the play will end happily instead of—she squeezed her head to clear it of horrors.

In the bedroom, the three were still sleeping. She started to pack things. They wouldn't need that much. She went to the main bedroom and dragged down the bag of Christmas gifts, Brenny's dump truck, the Wonderman for Jace, and the little things for the baby. She found a duffle bag that just held everything in the bottom of Mrs Hennessy's wardrobe. She looked in the bathroom cabinet for toothpaste and soap. She saw something else there, and took it, too. Brenny, surprised and sleepy on his way to the bathroom, wondered why Leece had Mum's sleeping tablets in her hand.

They left the house very early, almost with the sunrise. The twins were wild with excitement and Charmaine was still drowsy. Lisa carried the heavy baby and the duffle bag, while the twins carried the other bags. There was no wind at all. At the corner she left the children standing while she deliberately crossed the road to look back at them as they stood near the graffiti fence. From here the words stood out, tall and clear. 'If suffering gave off smoke,' she read, 'the world would be covered in a thick, black pall.' She returned to the children and they made their way through the quiet early-morning streets to the train. Sydney in the east was covered with a thick dark smog. Lisa knew why now.

'We're going to the beach!' rejoiced Brenny. 'We're going to stay at the beach house!' And Jace skipped along beside him, pleased and proud to have such a holiday in front of them. There was the excitement of the old train at Central, one with luggage racks and corridors and toilets, and they wriggled around, first wanting to sit here, then there; running up and down the side aisle until Lisa had to be stern with them and make them sit down and behave. Sydney was heating up but the moving air fanned them. Charmaine went to sleep after watching wide-eyed for half an hour as the southern suburbs slipped away. But the boys became cross and argumentative.

'Look, Leece. He's sitting on my towel and he won't give it back.'

'Give it back, Brenny.'

'It's mine, Leece. Look. It's got that bit of paint on it.'

'Brenny, you know it's mine.'

She tried to distract them. 'Look. Look at the oysters growing.'

'Oor, yuck. I hate oysters.'

'Yuck, so do I.'

'Are we there yet?'

'No. We're not.'

'Well, are we nearly there?'

'Oh, I don't know. For goodness' sake, Brenny, will you stop getting at me!'

This was so unexpected, and the tone of Lisa's voice so odd and harsh, that Brenny stared at her, open-mouthed.

It was getting hotter, and even the easterly, her pure wind, seemed now corrupted. Through the windows it pressed on them, humid and enervating, until their skin stuck to the train seats.

'How much further, Leece?'

'About half an hour. How about putting your heads down and having a nap? You were late last night. You're both tired and cranky.'

'I am not cranky.'

'Yes, you are.'

'I'm not. Anyway, you're real cranky, too.'

Brenny looked away in disgust and sulked for a while. But his natural good humour and the idea of the beach holiday soon cheered him. Charmaine woke up and announced 'Wee-wee' with a red face. Lisa helped her down the swaying corridor and into the narrow toilet compartment. The baby was fascinated by the small, silver toilet. 'Wee-wee!' she roared with delight as Lisa lifted her on.

Charmaine hung on grimly as the train rattled south. Lisa wiped her bottom and lifted her off. She helped her wash her hands in the little low basin and gently made her put back the miniature soap. She staggered back up the corridor with Charmaine lurching from side to side, Lisa grabbing her when necessary. 'Wee-wee train!' cried Charmaine to the boys, who cringed with embarrassment.

And finally they were there. Lisa decided to get a taxi and the twins both wanted to sit in the front. Then they both wanted to sit in the back. At the house, she paid the cab-driver from her small reserve and told them not to run around to the back but made them wait while she unpacked their stuff. 'We'll go down in a minute, I promise, if you'll just hold on.'

'Please, Leece. Please hurry up. I'm so hot I'm like a desert.'

'Me too, Leece. I'm as hot as hot.'

Charmaine looked around her, slowly turning her head

like an old woman's as she wondered at the strange lino, the alien walls and furniture.

'Just wait a minute longer while I have a cup of tea.'

'Yuck, I hate tea. Please, can we go down now?'

'No. It's too dangerous. You just wait a minute longer.' She drank her tea with the children staring at her, as if she might disappear in a flash. Then, when she put down the cup, they bolted away in front of her.

'Get back!' she screamed. 'The cliff's just there! You'll fall over.' Brenny halted and peered down. She was right. There *was* a cliff. He craned over.

'Wow!' he breathed, reverently. He pushed a hand behind him to stop Jace coming any closer.

'Look, Jace.' Down below, the water surged around the black rocks in jade and silver florals. A spout blew up glittering, to hang for a second before collapsing. Brenny followed the line of rocks with his eyes and saw the beach below.

'There it is, Jace! Leece, there's our own beach. The one you told us about. A beach all of our own.' He turned, begging. 'Oh, please can we go down now?'

Lisa smiled and they whooped away from her. They made their way down the cliff track, hanging in against the hillside. On their right, the waves crashed below them and Brenny shivered to think of falling, falling through the air and on to the black rocks. At the bottom of the track the sand began. It was very hot underfoot but there was a low green creeper that criss-crossed the sand near the cliff and they trod on that as far as it went. The boys howled and ran into the water. Lisa picked Charmaine up but the baby wanted to follow her brothers and screamed with rage.

'It's all right, Sharms, I'm taking you in. The sand's too hot for your feet.' But Charmaine was furious and only quietened when she was set down on the firm damp sand. She took off, swaying and wobbling, splashing and squealing through the lacy foam, utterly fearless. A big wave smacked her over and she looked around, wondering whether to cry or not. But just then, the out-rushing water drifted sand and a spray of seaweed over her toes and she kicked her feet with joy.

Lisa sat further up the beach where she could see them safely. Her heart was full of love for the three small bodies that played in the surf. Gulls wheeled overhead. She lay back, leaning an elbow in the sand. She would give them the most beautiful party on Christmas Eve, and before that, the most beautiful beach holiday of their lives. They would never enjoy themselves so much as they would these last few days.

She made a barbecue for them that night, using the griller from Uncle Doug's old stove over a small fire. The twins minded the sausages very seriously and Charmaine loved to watch the sparks of fire flickering upwards. Across the sea, the twilight glowed under the water until the sky and ocean seemed to be made of the same translucent rose jade. Then far-away lights, like stars, shone across the water, while overhead, real ones emerged. They tried to number them at first, lying on their backs on the grass, shouting at each new one. But then they were suddenly visible in such huge numbers that the boys went silly trying to count them.

'One milliony-milliony-milliony!' screamed Brenny, rolling over in excitement. And Charmaine squealed at her brothers.

Later, as Brenny threw scraps out for the gulls, he was drawn to the cliff. He leaned forward, trying to see where it was. Something loomed up behind him and he screamed. Then laughed with relief. It was only Leece.

That night, long after the children had gone to sleep, Lisa sat on the back step as the pound and surge of the sea flowed through her body. There was a sort of peace, now that she'd finally made up her mind. She was sure, now, that all the dreadfulness was coming to an end. And that somewhere there was another world, peaceful like the dream kindergarten. She and the children would live there for ever, playing on the crystal tower above the clouds. The lions would never be able to reach up there.

She stood up and walked warily nearer the cliff. The surf roared and paused in crashing sequences, impelled by the heartbeat of the tides and winds. She wondered at its vastness and black invisibility. It had always been there and always would be. 'Eternal' the waves seemed to repeat, then sigh. She could feel her own beating heart and it seemed to keep time with the swing of the sea. She remembered her days with Leila as their bodies rose and fell over the fence near the tree, the air rushing past the swings and lifting their hair, the chant of cicadas and the roar of the air in her ears so like this huger sound. She had been happy then, before she had found out about things so full of pain that the heart hurt to know of them and their hatefulness. But now she could restore peace to herself and to the children who would never have to know. She imagined drowning, twirling helplessly and soundlessly under millions of tons of black water, even though she was standing safely above the sea surrounded with peaceful air and the night closing softly about her.

Mrs McGregor watched as Lisa chose items from the shop. A frozen turkey, cranberry sauce, a tin of plum pudding, cream, a bottle of red cordial, vegetables, sweets, bon-bons, paper hats and party whistles.

'Having a party, dear?'

Lisa nodded.

'Won't you be going home for Christmas?'

The girl nodded again and Mrs McGregor didn't like to ask any more questions. She counted up the items and Lisa paid and left the shop.

'It seems a bit odd, don't you think, Ernie, that Lisa's got those kids with her? She's very young to have all that responsibility. You'd think they'd be home with their mother this close to Christmas.'

Ernest grunted and went on cleaning the freezer shelves. Outside, Brenny and Jace argued about who would carry what and Charmaine grabbed at the paper bag, crushing one of the whistles.

Two more splendid summer days were to follow; days as brilliant as blue-white diamonds; sand so hot it burned the instep, yet an easterly so crisp you could sometimes shiver in it. In the mornings, they would wind down the cliff track, the two boys daring to go ahead while Lisa struggled with the baby, and every day Charmaine screamed in rage thinking she would be left out. When the boys reached the sand, they would drop their towels and run to the surf, yelling with joy. Lisa would set the baby down on the sand and watch while she staggered to the water's edge, laughing, with the tears still running down her cheeks. Lisa would sit herself down on a towel and watch them until she was stupefied with the glare of the sand and the sea. After a few hours, Charmaine would be blue-lipped and bravely shivering. Lisa would wrap her up and yell at the boys, who would climb unwillingly back to the house for quick showers and some lunch.

They wanted her to let them go down by themselves, but she never would, saying it was too dangerous. So they'd sit around whingeing while she leafed through a magazine, or listened to music while Charmaine had her sleep. She made them promise not to go down to the beach without her. But they were allowed to play in an old cement pillbox that Brenny had discovered near the cliff path, an old grey square, its flooring split with thistles and small shrubs. They played soldiers and fights, and Brenny explained to Jace how Hogan's heroes and the people from *MASH* had stopped the Germans from getting to Australia in a big fight at Gallipoli.

But Brenny was worrying. Lisa seemed so different these days. He looked back at her, where she sat on her towel. She always just sat there, she never played with them any more, the way she used to. Just sat there in the same old place looking at them. Maybe she was just turning into a grown-up and getting boring like grown-ups were. She had bosoms like a lady. It was a pity, thought Brenny. He would never get boring, he decided. He would go to the pictures every night and for dinner he'd have cake-mix, much nicer uncooked, and then ice-cream and caramel sauce and then chocolates.

It was funny, he thought, that grown-ups, who could do anything they wanted to, never did anything like that. They ate spinach and stuff, and even cooked it for themselves. He would have a job and play with Jace at night and stay up very late and watch anything he wanted to on television.

He rushed up behind Jace who was facing out to sea waiting for a wave, and grabbed him round the waist, rolling over and over with him in the surf as they were dumped. Then he wandered up to Lisa and sat near her, not speaking, and making little tunnels for his feet in the sand, or piling dry sand into peaks over his toes. The day, although so bright, was misty near the beach; countless tiny drops hung in the air refracting light. He spoke softly and without looking up.

'Why are you so sad, Leece?'

He raised his eyes to hers and saw something in her face that he couldn't understand. She turned her eyes away from his and stared out to sea.

'Because I love you,' she finally replied.

Brenny flung himself away and hurtled down to the water. Tomorrow was Christmas Eve and the day after that—if Leece had been her old self, he couldn't have been happier. His stomach squeezed with delight when he thought of a dump truck. It had a lever and when you pressed it, the entire back of the truck started to tilt all by itself. You could put sand in it, or rocks. He could build roads and dams with it in the backyard and it would be just like the real one he'd seen across the street at the Daleys' place when they did their extension.

II

Verity was so late for their dinner appointment that Helen was about to leave the restaurant unfed when her friend rushed up to her and kissed her, very bright-eyed.

'I'm so sorry, darling. The traffic was dreadful.'

They ordered curries and chutney, poured wine from a flagon. The meal was good and they needed the cold riesling in quantities. Finally, Helen tilted the flagon. 'Do you realise, Vee, that between us, we've just about knocked it over?'

'Hardly felt a thing,' laughed Verity, lighting a cigarette. 'And if I get lonely over Christmas, can I come over for a day or two?'

'Of course.'

'Richard's going north. I'll be on my own. He's running around borrowing fishing tackle at the moment.' She grabbed her friend's hand. 'Helen, I've got some news. I think I know where she is.'

'Jumbo?'

Verity looked blank, then her face cleared. 'No. No, the other one. My lost girl. I'm not sure—it's all on touch and feel. I went to see the people at Jigsaw today and—oh, I'll have to go back to explain. The Department has to be so careful. They can't betray the anonymity of the adoptive parents. But many of them are women, and mothers. They'll let you have crumbs. You've no idea how comforting crumbs can be when you're starving. They'll give you hints, the child's new first name. Sometimes they try to reassure you by telling you how financially secure the family is, perhaps even mention that Dad is an accountant—things like that. They might mention a lovely suburb. Of course, it's not all done at once, but after many years, you get to build up a profile. They'd be frightened, I think, if they realized how much they give away. Come back for a nightcap—that's if we can still walk—and I'll show you what I've got.'

Sixteen years, Verity was thinking in the cab. Sixteen years of obsession. The first statement that made up the Perdita dossier had been when the baby was taken from her. 'Cheer up,' the sister had said. 'It's all for the best. She's going to a lovely Catholic couple on the coast.' The words had etched themselves; they burned through all the tears, pain and bitterness, the remorse and guilt. The silly rhythm of the phrase, the absurd alliteration had had her in hysterics more than once over the years. But there'd been little more about the lovely couple on the coast, although Verity had developed a radar in connection with her daughter that constantly scanned. They'd called her Vanessa. They would, Verity had grimly thought at the time. And it had been a clue. It wasn't an old-fashioned Catholic name, of the sort you can tell at a glance; Majella, Imelda, Gemma, Dominica. Or the first-born son of a difficult labour, Gerard. Although what on earth Gerard would have known about labour, difficult or otherwise, was an amusing mystery to Verity. Vanessa was a Protestant name, almost a debbie name. Perhaps the lovely Catholic couple were converts, or the new father part of the upwardly mobile lot who no longer voted Labour on instinct; endless theories to tease out there. She went to the bottom drawer of her desk, drew out the folder and handed it to Helen.

'You see, no one ever tells you anything straight out. It's not deliberate coyness or deceit. I think it must come from long years of trying to be humane—but drawing a line somewhere. And you've got to remember that this business works two ways. I've heard the most heart-breaking stories of kids who've finally tracked down their real mothers. And it's not uncommon for the mother to turn on them, deny them. Tell them they never want to hear from them again —that as far as they are concerned the child is dead. I wonder what that does to you? Particularly when you understand the obsession as well as I do. One kid haunted cemeteries for years, every school holidays, all weekends, trying to find her mother's grave. She'd been told the mother had died having her.'

'Poor little kid,' said Helen sadly.

'And then there are the ones who think they must have been bad and their mothers gave them away because of that. Or they live in constant fear of being given away again, because it happened once before.' Verity thought of how it must be for a child, to live in that world of half-truth and denial. Or the taunts about what sort of woman their mother must have been.

'And yet it's nobody's fault. It's not those women's fault that terror makes them cruel. They might have gone on and made another life for themselves—other children, a husband who'd be horrified rather than sympathetic. The lives they've so painfully reconstructed for themselves might all be destroyed by the truth. It's easy to blame them. Too easy.'

Helen looked up from the folder. 'I had no idea,' she said, 'that you'd do this.'

Verity laughed shortly. 'It's an obsession. I can't help it. And I'm getting closer. I've got a surname. It might have been the name of the officer in charge of the case or it mightn't have been anything to do with anything. I read it upside down from the file. And then I looked it up in the phone book. And Helen, there *is* one. There's an Irvine who's an accountant in the town where I'm sure she lives.'

'What are you going to do?'

Verity shook her head slowly. 'Honestly, I have no idea. One woman I know of has known her son's house for years. She just parks the car there and sits watching the house. Sometimes she sees him—at least, she thinks it's him—coming in or out. I really don't know.'

'You'd have to be very sensitive.'

'Yes. Hard for me.'

'Nonsense,' laughed Helen. 'And another thing's just occurred to me.'

'What's that?'

'How do you know your daughter isn't working on one of these—' she indicated the folder—'herself? She might even track you down before you find her.'

Verity looked stunned. 'I'd never thought of that.'

'Good heavens, why not? She's your daughter, Verity Unicombe.'

Yes, indeed she is, thought Verity after she'd seen Helen out. And what *did* she think she'd do herself? You can't bowl up to a strange young girl and say, 'Hi, I'm your real mum.' Nor could she ring. Perhaps a letter to the adoptive mother? She poured a small whisky, lit a cigarette and sat at the table with pen and paper.

'Dear Mrs Irvine,' she wrote, 'I hope my writing to you is not too much of a shock.' Stupid, she thought, and crossed that out. 'I know this letter will be something of a shock.' She paused. What am I doing? she asked herself. Why can't I just wait another two years until my girl's eighteen? I've endured sixteen.

But she continued writing. 'I would so like to see my daughter. I understand that this might be very upsetting for her.' For her, for me, and for you, adoptive mother. Her teacher's mind started working. She'll go into year 11 next year, then the Higher School Certificate. Isn't it very important that things be calm on the home front through these difficult years? The intrusion of one's natural mother would upset even the most phlegmatic adolescent. And how many of those are there?

No. She couldn't do it. Be patient, she argued with herself. I'm not even sure that I really want to see her or whether the Jumbo business has churned everything up again. It is very hard, she thought, to compare the urgency of one time with the urgency of the present. It might be that I'm quite happy to relinquish my daughter because I fear my own capacity to mother.

She picked up her pen again. 'I have very confused thoughts about this matter. Perhaps you would be good enough to write to me and assure me that all is well.' But she stopped. What if all is not well? What if Perdita had died in a car crash, or had been attacked and murdered in the National Park or had run away a year ago and was shooting up in a squat? Do I want to hear that? It might be better to cherish the illusion of my family on the coast where Perdita comes home straight after school, does four hours of homework then gracefully washes up after a marvellous and nourishing meal. Perhaps even reads stories to her younger 'siblings', then retires without fuss at half past ten so as to be fresh for music practice at seven next morning. Why not leave well alone? Who needs more complications in their lives?

'I do not wish to intrude upon your life and the life of your family, but it is dreadful not knowing.' She thought of all the tragic mothers of missing children, holding up the beloved's photograph for the press or television; the pathetic pleas to the torturers. She tore the letter into tiny pieces. She went to the window that reflected her approach. She stood very near the glass and cupped a hand over her eyes to see outside. The stars shone in a cloudless sky and the mountains in the west seemed to huddle closer and hotter than usual. It is just the booze, she told herself, that has created this dreadful yearning; the cup that cheers for a while then reveals the hollowness, the dark sadness at the heart of things. Maudlin fool, she told herself and drew the heavy curtains. She looked around the comfortable, well-furnished room; the books collected through two and a half degrees, the paintings, the handwoven rugs, the pale woollen carpet. She had everything necessary for a decent life. And she was wasting it, in fact. Allowing herself to be eaten away with remorse and guilt. She should be like Helen, self-contained and content, pleased with her job, her life and her cat. She switched off the lamp and went to bed where sleep ambushed her suddenly into unconsciousness.

Tom Bennett was surprised to hear her voice, Verity thought. And pleased. Yes, of course he'd meet her for a drink. He knocked off at three—was that any good? That was fine. They met at the riverside hotel, and in the air-conditioned lounge they watched the sun beating down on the outside timber decking. Below it, the flat river made its slow, brown way to the east. Now that she was here, Verity was suddenly self-conscious.

'How have you been?' she asked awkwardly.

'Not too bad.' He glanced at her quickly. 'I saw Pam last night. We had a talk. Well, no. More of a fight, really.' He didn't volunteer any more and Verity didn't like to ask further.

'I'll keep my fingers crossed,' she said.

'Thanks.'

After a pause, she straightened her shoulders and continued. 'I've been wondering, Tom, if you could advise me.' His light blue eyes met hers. 'It's not really a police matter, but I thought—'

'Go on,' he encouraged.

She breathed deeply. 'Sixteen years ago, I had a baby girl. And she was adopted out. I've managed to gather a bit of information over the years.'

'I see.' Tom Bennett considered. 'Have you thought of a private detective? That might be the answer.' The speed and accuracy of his surmise pleased her.

'Could you recommend one?'

The fair man considered again. Then he shook his head. 'Not round here. There are a couple of local blokes, but one's a drunk and the other's a fool. But I could ask. I know there are good ones. It's just a matter of knowing who.' He swallowed his drink. 'They don't come cheap, you know.'

Verity nodded. 'I'm not even sure if I'll do it. It's just a thought I had. Do you want another whisky?' But he shook his head.

'No, thanks all the same. I'd better be getting back to the girls. Mum's flat out at the moment—Christmas and everything. I was hoping Pam would be back for Christmas. I mucked everything up last night.' He looked steadily at her. 'She'd agreed to come over for Christmas dinner so that we could all be together. And then she asked me how I'd manage cooking my first turkey. She was smiling and it made me furious. I told her that Mum was cooking it and that seemed to make her furious. So that's where it ended with me walking out of her place.'

'Her place?'

'Yeah. She's got a little hole of a place. I don't know how she can stand to live there. She's down off Station Street. Looks like it should be condemned.'

'So she's not with the tennis coach?'

'No. She says that's over. That it wasn't important. Christ! She can leave her kids, leave a marriage and then tell me it's not important!'

Verity was silent for a while.

'Perhaps she means that that isn't the issue—that there are other problems—that the tennis coach was just, say, a symptom of something else.'

He nodded. 'I think I can see that when I'm not so angry. I know what she means then. And she's right, too. Things haven't been so good between us for a while now.' There followed a silence until he looked up again. 'I'm so bloody confused. Sometimes I feel like giving her a swift kick up the backside and telling her to make her own bloody arrangements. Other times I want to almost beg her to come back.' Once again, he showed that surprising grin. 'Neither one's very rational, is it?'

'Try the middle way.' Verity smiled. 'She probably needs a bit of time.'

Tom Bennett frowned. 'That's the hardest bloody thing to give anyone.'

'I know that,' Verity replied, thinking of a painful time between herself and Richard. 'It is the hardest thing in the world to give.'

'And there's still the kids,' he continued. 'They're still in the dark. They don't know what's happening. I could nearly cry when they ask when is Mum coming home and I can't help them. They're trying to be so good for me. It'd break your heart.' He put his drink down. 'I just wish I knew what to do. Thanks for listening to all this. It's a relief just to talk about it.' They left the lounge and she turned to him.

He stood looking at her for a minute as if he might say something, then thanked her again and hurried away.

Verity ripped the envelope open. There was no address; just the big loopy letters, the circles over the *i*s. She read it. Then covered her mouth with her hands as if she might scream. Richard grabbed it.

'What'll we do?'

Suddenly he was taking it as seriously as she always had. 'We'd better take it to the police.'

'And tell them what?' Verity whispered. 'I don't even know—I can't tell them anything.'

'Stop blaming yourself, Vee.' He put the letter down and his arm around her. 'Look. Tell the experts—that's what they're there for—put it in their hands and then come away with me. You'll have done everything humanly possible. No one could do any more.'

'I can't go anywhere now, don't you see? I've got to find this child. If I don't, she'll think I don't care and she'll do this terrible thing. I'm her confidante. I can't let her down.'

Richard's arm dropped from her waist.

'You're not being rational,' he said harshly. 'This isn't a second chance. This isn't your daughter all over again.' She raised stricken eyes to his, but he walked to the bedroom and turned to her at the door.

'I'm going to start packing now. I'd like you to come with me.'

She didn't answer. She rang Helen.

'Ring Tom Bennett. I'm on my way.'

When Verity heard the telephonist say, 'Hold the line, please,' she nearly dropped with relief. He was there. He'd know what to do. 'It's me, Verity,' she said in answer to his question. 'No. This is something quite different. I've had a letter. I've had three letters, actually. But this one—' She stopped. 'I'm not making much sense.'

Tom Bennett's voice was interested, even urgent. 'Never mind,' he said. 'Just go on. Just tell me.'

She did the best she could. 'And the worst of it is, that I've lost the first one, the one with the address.'

'Bring the other two down with you. Have one last look for that first one. And the envelopes.'

She did. She ransacked the kitchen. She tore through all the crevices and crannies that letters can hide in. She pulled open books, shook magazines, looked behind cupboards and rifled the glove box and under the car seats. She found things she'd lost and couldn't turn up months ago. But nowhere did she find that childish writing with the little circles over the i's. She was almost crying when Helen arrived.

Together they went to the police station. Bennett was waiting for her near the reception desk. She sat in his office and told him the whole thing again. As she was speaking, he listened intently, his eyes fixed on her, sometimes nodding shortly. He then read the two letters over, frowning.

'And you have no idea at all who this young person is?'

Verity pressed her hands together in her lap. 'None at all. It's someone I must have taught in sixth grade. She's—'

'Why do you assume it's a she?'

'The babysitting. The letters. Boys don't generally write.'

'Yes. It's more likely to be a girl. But we mustn't assume. This nickname, this Jumbo—does nothing come to mind?'

Verity shook her head.

'This is what I want you to do. I want you to get hold of the school records or whatever you keep—class rolls—yearly photographs—that sort of stuff, and go through them carefully. Try and remember everything you can about every one of them. The name Jumbo is very important to this young person. Although she—or he—is hiding behind it, it must mean something to her—something that you know. She wouldn't have used it otherwise.'

'Do you think, Tom,' she asked slowly, 'that something happened, I mean between Jumbo and me, that was enormously important to her?'

'I do. And when you remember it, we've got her.'

Verity's mind was spinning; a crazy ferris-wheel of faces, voices, memories, the idiosyncracies of thousands of students. So many moments of love and anger, curiosity, affection, sorrow. 'There are so many of them. There are thousands of them.'

'There's only one Jumbo. And until we know who it is, we can do nothing about the threats.'

'But someone, somewhere, is missing three kids! She must be frantic.'

'Not necessarily. Jumbo babysits, remember. She might be in a position of trust. The mother might be anywhere. That's my job if the woman contacts us. Let me worry about that. Your job is to remember who Jumbo is. I can do everything else after that.'

After the two women had left his office, Tom Bennett lowered his eyes to the letter again: 'Dear Miss, I can't stand it any more. I love these kids too much to let them know about all the terrible things I know about. I'll give them a wonderful Christmas at the beach and then we'll all go to sleep and be safe for ever.'

Verity and Helen were surrounded on the floor with class rolls, school photos, pupil record cards and everything they could think of that might cover the year, or years of Jumbo. Richard, carrying a suit case, looked at them in silence, then left the house. Verity, torn, ran outside. He was putting the case into the boot.

'I'm going now,' he said, but his voice was gentle.

'Yes. But you know I can't.'

'No. I know. But I don't want you to think—'

'Look, it's all right.'

They looked at each other with a new tenderness.

'I hope you find what you're looking for, Vee.' She closed her eyes and nodded. They didn't kiss. Verity felt something had finished between them. An old fight? An old secret? She went back inside. There had been a second's vigorous temptation, when she'd longed to feel his familiar arms around her, hear his heart beating. He was right. She had done what she could. But she knew there was more. The job of recognizing Jumbo in all of those possible names and smiling or squinting faces now awaited her and she turned to her work with an unfamiliar prayer.

12

It was a perfect summer afternoon and the children sat around the table making Christmas decorations. Lisa had made a Christmas tree—not a proper one, thought Brenny—out of a branch and now they were helping to make the chains and stars for it. Brenny coloured in a star. Leece had drawn the outline for him. This was good fun because if you went over the lines, it didn't matter because you cut it out anyway. Jace was grunting with effort beside him, and Sharmers was sitting on the floor and playing with some stuff—glitter was its name—and she had glittery fingers and a glittery mouth and chin because she'd tried to eat it, but had screwed up her face like the day she had eaten some sand. Little kids always have to try and eat everything, Brenny thought.

'Leece is different,' he said softly to Jace beside him.

'A bit.'

They went on with their work. The room was starting to look pretty good. Leece had made some streamers to loop along the mantelpiece and there were cut-out bits of Christmas cards along the edge—people in fur-lined cloaks looking into glowing shop windows, starry nights and snow, a Father Christmas with a big bag of toys. And the shot-gun was missing off the wall. As if he couldn't notice that. He'd been longing to get that gun down for days. But when he'd asked Leece to get it down for him, she'd yelled at him. Girls hated guns. You could see the outlines on the wall of the two guns now. Like two ghost guns. Uncle Doug must have taken the other one with him, because when they'd first got there, Brenny had noticed one gun and one gun's outline. That was one of the things that was bothering him. There were others, like how come they were having Christmas here when they should be at home. They should be putting up the proper decorations, the big honeycombed paper bells that turned out fat as pineapples when you pinned them back. It was nice here, and the beach was terrific, but really, they should be getting home so that they could all be there when Mum and her friends opened that fizzy wine and they all laughed a lot and Mum said she was a bit tiddly. These decorations were fun to make and everyone seemed happy, but he was worried.

'Leece?'

'Mmm?'

'Leece, I think we should go home now.'

Lisa didn't reply. She just kept drawing more of the star outlines. Mrs Unicombe had taught her how to make a chain of stars in sixth class. Jace looked up and echoed his brother's concern.

'Yes, Leece. Let's go home now.'

Charmaine studied each of her brothers and started to cry.

'Mumma, Mumma!' she bellowed, rubbing glitter into her eyes and screeching harder.

Lisa swept her up and turned on the boys. 'Now look what you've done! You've got Sharmers all upset! There, darling Sharms, darling Sharms,' and she danced the crying child around the room. Charmaine quietened and Lisa turned from her dancing.

'Well, we can't go home because it's Christmas and there's no trains.'

'But Mum'll be worried. She'll come home and no one will be there.' Brenny's voice wobbled.

'She's coming here, silly. It's supposed to be a surprise and that's why I didn't tell you yet.'

Jace grinned but Brenny kept colouring in without looking at her. 'She doesn't know how to get here.'

'I told her. I rang her up from the shop and told her. And she said you could open your presents tonight as a special surprise.'

'Wow!' breathed Jace. Brenny didn't answer. He was not

pleased. You opened your presents on Christmas Day, he was thinking, very early in the morning when it's still a little bit dark. You don't open them any other time.

'I don't want to.'

'I do.'

'You're silly, Jace.'

'I am not.'

'I'm not going to open my presents till the proper time.'

He thought a bit longer.

'How will Mum get here?'

'On the train.'

'Mumma!' squealed Charmaine. 'Wee-wee train!' Brenny glanced at her scornfully. Little babies believed anything.

'When did you talk to Mum?'

'I've already told you. I rang her from the shop when you and Jace and Sharmers were outside.'

Brenny didn't argue. He knew she was lying. Her face had that angry look that people get when they're telling lies and they know you don't believe them. Jace was still colouring in, with his head on one side pretending he didn't care. But even he, thought Brenny, must have spotted the lie about the train.

Lisa sat on the back step clutching a cup of cold tea. She stared out to sea. A few gulls wheeled and dived, pure white against the haze of the horizon. Northwards, she could see the black outcrop of the coast stretching away, toy houses half hidden in the dark eucalypt clumps. The sea was mild today, the far nesses only ruffled about with white, no waves exploding over them. A few fishing boats drifted near shore, and further out, so that its colours were drained, a grey tanker inched its way over the thin line dividing sky and sea. Christmas, she was thinking. You can tell it's Christmas by the air, by the heat of the sun and by the colours of the bush. Behind the house, near the road, fire-blackened trees stood in clumps. Low-lying coastal scrub huddled under them and a few kangaroo tails thrust their spears into the air. And there were flowers all around of different shades of yellow, from cream to chrome. Some of the scrubby bushes were two-toned, lighter at the tips like cypress. Ahead of her, the wild hedge near the cliff was covered with flowers, savage-looking blooms with black in their hearts. You could just tell, she was thinking, by all this that it was Christmas time.

Those awful Christmas dinners, hot and heavy meat that you ate with the sweat on your face. Uncle Cass and Aunt Merle. She hadn't seen them in years. Cass had died and Merle, remarried, had gone to live in another state. The Christmas of the pink and white bikini had been the day, Lisa was thinking, that her father had turned away from her. 'What did I do wrong?' she whispered. Only a gull screeched, attacking one of its brothers, and they fell squabbling below the line of her vision under the cliff. And her friend Leila. What had happened to her? Had she gone the way of Nancy or would she go into domestic servitude with kids—or was she even alive? Leila had dumped her like everyone else. Her father, Mrs Hennessy. Only the kids loved her. She went to the edge of the cliff and tossed the cold tea over, watching its amber brilliance disappear. The gulls swept after it, but pulled back, disappointed. A sudden terror surged through her body, stiffening her. She fumbled in her pocket for one of the tiny blue tablets that Dragon had given her. She swallowed its bitterness and waited on the step for its magic to work. In a little while, her muscles loosened, but the fear crouched in her guts and waited.

Lisa checked the turkey. She basted it slowly, carefully. All her movements seemed oddly slow and measured since she'd taken a few more of Dragon's pills. 'Take some of these,' he'd said to her, 'when you're hurting. You won't feel anything for a while.' And it was true. Nothing hurt now. Not even when she'd burnt her hand on the hot oven. She'd looked at her hand and watched while it turned a slow red.

She distributed the sweets into little glass dishes and, when those ran out, into saucers. She opened a packet of nuts into a wooden platter that she'd found under the sink. She'd washed the cherries and put them on plates. Long stripes of evening sun slanted across the newly swept room. The streamers and stars that the kids had made stirred softly as you went past them. And the Christmas tree looked beautiful. Several bumpy packets stood under it. Lisa had made an angel to go on the top, another lesson from sixth grade. From here it looked good, but it was really only a peg, a hankie and some cellophane.

Charmaine was chewing very quietly. 'Oh no, Sharmers! You can't. Look what she's doing, Leece.' The baby had stuffed several toffees into her mouth, paper and all, and was uncomfortably trying to chew them.

Lisa prised them from the sticky gums and tiny teeth while Charmaine roared. 'Look, Sharms, you've got to take the paper off, see?' As Lisa untwisted a wrapper, the baby was all attention, pointing and smiling to see the toffee revealed. 'See?' But then she became perverse and hurled the toffee across the floor, yelling. Jace laughed and pounced on it.

Lisa picked up the baby and went to the back door with her. The brilliant blue of the sky was deepening to prussian; the blinding white of the gulls' feathers toned to apricot in the low sun. Charmaine followed their wheeling and swooping with hypnotized eyes. Now the sea was empty; no ships, no white horses. There was little texture on its surface and at the horizon it was merely a denser colour than the powdery mauve of the sky.

If only I could keep them all safely here, away from horrible schools and horrible people who would hurt them, she thought. And never, never let them know about the terrible things. But it was impossible. Her earlier dream of them all living here was silly; a stupid, childish dream. The dinner cooking in the oven had cost her the only bit of money she had in the world.

She rocked Charmaine to her. Behind her, the boys were busy with their special Christmas cards for each other. Now that it was getting nearer, there was a calmness she hadn't felt before. Nothing seemed real any more. Not even herself.

Even the memory of the Unicorn was fading. She could never have cared for Lisa either. That day had been a lie; all false and cut out. Would she even remember, the Unicorn, when she read of what was going to happen here? How would it be reported? 'Four found dead in beach shack.' These words had a heavy sound to them. But they sounded right, as if they should be printed. And it would be easy. They must feel no pain, the children. Nor must they be afraid. They must not, in their last minutes, suffer like the poor people and the beasts. No, she would make sure of that. Like stars in the morning they would just go out, or like the tiny sea-snails swept out by a wave, they would make only the softest tinkle.

Charmaine scrambled off her lap. From inside the house, she could hear the murmuring of the twins as they worked, and then Charmaine's good-humoured ramblings, but in the pit of her stomach, the fear stirred momentarily as she hardened with terror. The bitter tablets still spread their mist through the channels of her body, and in a little while her knees loosened their knot and she was able to stand up. But a frightening tremor suddenly shivered through her thighs and she sat again. If only the Unicorn would come. Lisa felt stripped and racked, and, like a victim of the torturer, she longed for blackness.

She looked inside. Darling Sharmers was scrubbing her toffee into the carpet, singing to it and eating the fluff from it. Jace was still finishing his special secret cards for them all and Brenny was looking at her in a way that made her feel anger. But his eyes flickered away from her. She loved them so much, she thought. And soon they would be safe for ever.

13

Helen had poured them both a whisky and they sat in the mess of records, books and photographs. Verity looked up. Her face was drawn and pale.

'It's no use. It's just no use. My mind's a blank. I don't remember anyone called Jumbo.'

'Take it easy. Don't worry.' Helen's voice, gentle and strong.

Verity sipped her drink and blinked. 'I wonder,' she said, voicing the question that no one dared to frame, 'exactly how she plans to do it?'

'She mightn't, Vee. She mightn't even do it. It might be some horrible game she's playing.'

Verity shook her head. 'Oh, no. She'll do it all right. I can feel it in my bones. Tonight.'

Helen stood to stretch. 'I think we need a break. Let's go and have an early tea and then start again. You look whacked and I'm not much better.'

They walked to the local Chinese restaurant and found it almost empty. Christmas Eve is time for families, safe as houses, Verity was thinking. Somewhere, four young people were having Christmas Eve. And they would never see Christmas Day. Somewhere, her daughter was waiting to see what her sixteenth birthday would bring. They ate their meal in silence and Verity had to force down the tiny morsels while her throat and stomach rebelled at food's intrusion.

14

Sixty miles away, Lisa basted the turkey again. She could smell nothing, but in the room next door the kids sniffed in approval. She put it back in the oven. It reminded her of one of those stage props, of the sort of rigid food that gets thrown around in plays. She found a big boiler to heat the tinned plum pudding up in. Even though the evening was still hot, by the time the pudding had heated through, it might be cool enough to face it. She had found two threepences, a sixpence and a shilling in an old tobacco tin in a cupboard. She would press them into the childrens' slices. She pulled the jar of Mrs Hennessy's sleeping tablets out of her bag. Carefully, she cracked each capsule and poured the tiny grains into a cup. She had quite an amount there when she'd finished. She poured a little of the red cordial into the powder and stirred it well around. When it was dissolved, she tipped the viscous syrup into the cordial bottle and shook it up. Something made her turn and she saw Brenny watching her from the kitchen doorway.

15

Back in the mess on Verity's floor, the two friends drank coffee and despaired. It was almost eight o'clock.

'What I'm going to do,' said Helen in her matter-of-fact voice, 'is hand you the class photos and you're going to tell me everything you can remember about each kid. What they were like, what their parents were like. Everything. And then we'll move on to the next one.'

Despite everything, Verity laughed. 'You sound exactly as if you're speaking to 5E.'

Helen picked up one of the class photos, the one they both felt must have been Jumbo's year, and started with it.

'OK. From left to right. First girl in the back line, please.'

'That's Marika—Marika Somethingovsky—no, Lodovici. She was a good-humoured soul. Not what you'd call academically gifted. And that's Shawn beside her. He tried to be a surfie. Which is very hard forty miles inland. But he was a trier.' She looked up. 'I suppose I needn't worry about the boys.'

'Do them. You never know. It might set something off. Now, what about her? She's pretty overweight.'

'No. That's poor old Panzer. Pam Donohoe. Her dad died during that year and that's when she put on all that weight. Jumbo's dad been retrenched, remember. And that's Maria Cavelli—' She continued across the back line of children. Then she pointed to a narrow girl who started the middle row of pupils. 'And that's Lisa, little Lisa Brand. She was a funny one. Came to me in a flood of tears one day—' Verity raised her eyes; for a second she couldn't speak. Then she scrambled to her feet and rushed to the phone.

'Helen! That's her! That's Jumbo! Oh, where's Tom

Bennett's number? That's her!' She scrambled through the phone book with shaking fingers. 'Why is it,' she screamed, 'that government departments are so bloody well impossible to find?'

Helen pointed to the emergency number. 'Try that.' Verity dialled, spoke briefly and hung up.

'We'll go straight down to the police station with her photo and address. Quick.'

16

Now Brenny was frightened. All the things that had been worrying him seemed to have rolled themselves up into a heavy ball that now and then heaved over in his stomach. Leece, he had decided, must really be a witch. She must be a witch who got little kids. She'd put something in that red drink all right. And what was that great big pot of water doing on the stove? Leece must be going to poison them and cook them up like the witch in Hansel and Gretel. And all this time, she'd been tricking them, getting them to love her, just so she could eat them.

He looked over at her, and only half-believed his fear. There was Leece sitting quietly with Sharmers on her lap, singing some silly song to her. Leece wouldn't hurt them, would she? She loved them. But he was suddenly cold and wished himself and the others back safely at 73 Gardenia Crescent. He squeezed his eyes shut. When he opened them, they were still all at the beach house as he'd known they would be. He would have to think hard. He was the oldest by fifteen minutes and they all depended on him.

'Leece?'

'Mmm?' She slowly lifted her head from singing to Sharmers.

'Why have you got that big pot of water and nothing in it?'

'For the plum pudding.' She looked away again. Brenny slumped with relief. Things in tins have to be put in boiling water; he remembered that from home. Maybe the stuff in the red drink was some extra flavour or something.

'When do you think Mum'll get here?'

Once again, that slow turn, as if she didn't see him or even care that he was there.

'Later, tonight.'

And her voice was funny, like she was real sleepy, Brenny thought. He didn't like to ask her anything else. But she stood up and started to clear the table.

'Goody! Eats!' cried Jace. Charmaine crawled to a dish of sweets and crammed two more into her sticky mouth. Brenny went to help Lisa lay the table. He gave himself the special plate. The special plate had a picture of a man and a lady in old-fashioned clothes and behind them was a little boy sitting on a sleigh thing. Red rooftops could be seen in the distance over the pale hills. But Jace saw him.

'Leece. Brenny's having that plate again and you said I could have it next time.'

'Mmm?' Lisa frowned and went to pick up the plate. It slipped through her fingers and smashed on the floor. Brenny and Jace both stared at her and Jace started whingeing.

Lisa brought out the turkey, sizzling. Then she brought out the baked potatoes and set them down. There were more little dishes of sweets and cherries. Then she came out with the red drink in a big jug and three glasses. The table looked very nice. It was covered with pretty Christmas paper, there was a box of bon-bons, two dishes of nuts, a bowl of chocolates, and an angel made out of gold paper holding a little pretend candle. There were paper serviettes with holly and reindeers on them.

The meal looked beautiful. Witches didn't make nice dinners, Brenny thought, but then remembered with a chill about Hansel and Gretel. Brenny stared at the food that was being piled on to his replacement plate. He longed again for his mother. She could always tell him things. She knew when things on the telly were real and when they weren't real. Sometimes, she would laugh at him. 'Oh, Brenny,' she'd say, 'it's only a film. It's not real. Don't you worry.' He wished he had this skill. Perhaps then he'd be able to work out what was going on round here.

Why would Leece want to hurt them? She'd spent all her money taking them to this beach house and making this lovely party for them. But then, with a suddenness that made him catch his breath, he remembered his mother shaking her head in front of the telly with tears in her eyes. 'How could he do that?' she was saying. 'How could a man do that to his own little girl?' Dreadful things *did* happen. He desperately sought about for a reason. Wicked stepmothers! Perhaps Leece was one of those? They were ladies who pretended to be real mothers but hated children above all things and wanted to kill them very much. They were as nice as pie and then—pow! Maybe Leece was turning into one of those now that she was turning into a lady. Or, and this thought made him shiver despite the warm kitchen and the food he was eating mindlessly, maybe Mum was one? Wicked stepmothers always got someone else to take the children away, usually to a forest. He had never heard of a wicked stepmother who had used a beach house. Brenny knew of no way to tell a wicked stepmother from a proper one. Maybe Mum had wanted to get rid of them. She often complained about how much they cost to feed and stuff. 'If I didn't have you lot,' she used to say sometimes, 'I'd get a good education and a good job and drive a sports car.' But then she'd usually grab one of them and hug them like mad so that you knew she'd much rather have you than any of those other things. Sometimes she even said, 'I'll wring your neck, Brenny,' but you knew she didn't really mean it, that she really loved them all.

'Aren't you hungry, Brenny?' Leece was staring at him with those funny eyes. He shrugged and muttered something.

'You won't get any pudding unless you eat your proper dinner.' Her voice was so different, like a computer's voice, Brenny thought.

He stabbed at a baked potato. He bit it and chewed mechanically. But it wasn't just Mum any more, he was thinking. There was that rat man. Perhaps he was the one who wanted to get rid of them. He imagined Mum sitting on the lounge smoothing her gardenia and the rat man sitting beside her. 'Look, Bev,' he was saying, 'you are quite pretty and I would like to marry you but you'll have to get rid of the kids because kids cost too much money and I need all the money for my red car.' Men did not like kids much, as far as Brenny could see. His own dimly remembered father had left when Mum still had Sharmers inside her. He remembered awful fights and one time he remembered Mum lying on the floor crying because their father had hit her so hard. Mum used to say that all men are bastards. Why did she go out with that rat man?

Suddenly he froze. Lisa was pouring the red drink. She had placed one in front of Sharmers, one in front of him and one for Jace. Sharmers lunged for hers and Brenny jumped quickly, as if by accident, and knocked it to the floor. Charmaine started her red-faced bellow.

'Now look what you've done!' Leece was looking really mad. She picked up the fallen glass and Brenny looked at the awful red stain on the floor. She went to the kitchen. Brenny leaned across to his twin and whispered urgently.

'Why can't I?' Jace was asking as Lisa returned. 'Why not?'

'Just because.' Brenny's face was so pale and grim that Jace didn't argue. The four now sat in silence. Happy Charmaine, now that her new drink was on its way, painted part of her bib with cranberry sauce. Jace was watching the averted face of his brother; Lisa was bringing another red drink to the table. Outside, a gull shrieked. Sharmers made a grab for Jace's unattended glass and triumphantly drained it, chuckling over the rim at Brenny's stricken face.

Later, they collected the plates and took them to the kitchen. Brenny carried his red drink carefully to the sink and emptied it. As Leece followed in behind him, he smacked his lips theatrically. 'Dee-lishus,' he said as he put the empty glass near the sink. He went back for Jace's, and was horrified to see Lisa standing over his brother, wanting him to drink. Jace was looking from the one to the other in an agony of indecision. Brenny set his lips and willed his brother not to touch it. Lisa glared at the two of them. Jace's hand reached out uncertainly for the glass and with tears gathering in his eyes he looked at Brenny and raised the glass to his lips. He took a sip.

'Oor, yuck! This is awful, Leece.' And he pushed it aside, looking to his brother with relief.

'You drink it. Brenny loved his.'

'But it's yucky.'

'It is not. It's made of fruit and fruit is good for you. Drink it now.' There was something so threatening in her manner that Brenny watched with horror as Jace, his face screwed up, swallowed the drink.

'Good. And now you can all open your presents.' She was watching them intently. Jace, relieved to have pleased one of them, darted to the tree, then turned to Brenny, imploring him. But Brenny stood where he was, daring Jace to touch a present. If I can just keep the presents unopened, none of this will really be happening, he was telling himself. Jace walked to the back door and kicked it with frustration. Brenny's mind was racing. What could he do? They were both poisoned now. He despaired. Oh, please, God, he prayed hopelessly. Don't let this happen.

He looked to where his baby sister was talking softly to some cherries on the floor. His heart ached with love and hopelessness. 'Oh, Sharms,' he whispered and she lifted her head to look at him. Brenny was terrified by what he saw. Charmaine's mouth hung down like an idiot's and her lower lids sagged like a bloodhound's. Despite himself, he screamed. Lisa ran to see.

'Look! Look at Sharmers! What's happened?'

Lisa moved crookedly to pick up the baby.

'She's tired, that's all. Aren't you, darling Sharms?' She looked back at the twins.

'If you're not going to open your presents, you can all get to bed. You're all very, very tired, aren't you?'

There was an awful sound in her voice, as if she was about to scream and scream, thought Brenny. He was shocked into silence.

*

Brenny sat up in bed, his eyes wide open in the darkness. In the bed beside him, Charmaine snuffled. He swung his legs out and very quietly tiptoed across to the door. He could see through it a little, through the darkened living room and into the kitchen were Lisa was sitting. Her shadow fell across the worn rug. And there was something else, too. The long thing that cast a terrible shadow like a spear: the shot-gun. Brenny stood utterly still. It was as if he had found himself taking part in some horror show on the telly. He stood, transfixed, watching the shadows play horribly on the floor. So that was it. She wasn't only going to poison them, she was going to shoot them as well. He shivered all over. But then came a revelation. No. Sharmers and Jace weren't poisoned. Lisa had given them Mum's sleeping pills—that's why she'd put them in the red drink—to make them sleep so that when she came into the room later on they wouldn't wake up when she . . .

Brenny almost squeaked out loud with terror. He moved across to Jace in the dark room and shook his brother as hard as he could. 'Jace! Wake up! Wake up! You must wake up!' But his brother just rolled under Brenny's desperate hands like the drowned dog that they'd seen years ago, lolling in the surf, dead weight. Brenny held his breath. He put his ear close to Jace's mouth. Such slow, deep breathing as if it were coming from a long way away. A chair moved in the kitchen and Brenny jumped in terror. What was he going to do? But then there was silence. He'd have to get them out somehow. He'd have to get them somehow out of the window and down to the soldiers' cement place. Then, he thought, he could creep down to Mrs Mac's place and she could ring Mum and then Mum would come, thank God, and get them all.

Lisa sat quite still in the shabby kitchen. Outside, the sea sang and sighed. She put the gun carefully across the table. She stood four cartridges upright on the oilcloth. They gleamed, red and gold, like Christmas baubles, she thought. She felt at peace. The terrible idea no longer seemed terrible at all. It was right and good. Outside, the Pacific crashed blackly; right and good, it repeated, with every emphatic surge. No one loved in this world, it said. No one cared. But she did. She cared so much she would spare them all the cruelty and pain. She thought again of their brown bodies gleaming in the ice-blue surf; their squeals of delight as millions of salty diamonds showered them. Diamonds, ice-blue and the crystal palace of the Snow Queen on whose spire they would play for ever. She saw Brenny chasing his brother with a leafy rope of seaweed, trying to slap it against the other's narrow shoulders while Jace nearly choked with laughing and squealing and trying to run all together. And darling Charmaine, sitting square in the lacy shallows like a fat door-stopper, with the foam surging around her fat toes. Now they would never be touched by the thick black pall. And she too would be at peace.

If only the Unicorn had come, she thought with something like sadness. But the Unicorn hadn't cared. Once, Lisa had thought she had. That day when she'd been sobbing in the back of the classroom after everyone else had gone because the Unicorn had called her that awful name. And the Unicorn had come down to her and asked with such love and concern in her voice what was the matter. And Lisa had told her. Mrs Unicombe had taken out this most gorgeous hanky and wiped her tears away and made her blow her nose. ' "Disturbing element", is what I said. "Scurvy elephant" indeed! Come on, cheer up. I wouldn't call you an awful name like that.' And then Mrs Unicombe, instead of saying faintly that Lisa should keep the handkerchief, had gently taken it back, all snotty and teary as it was, patted her head and said, 'Now run along, little Jumbo.' And Lisa had been so moved she'd fallen in love with her on the spot. The Unicorn loves me, she'd often thought to herself. And the Unicorn only loves someone very pure in heart. But the Unicorn hadn't cared. She'd been even worse by pretending that she had. She was a false Unicorn. There were no such things, anyway. Lisa didn't sigh at this thought as once she would have. She was empty and numb and nothing hurt any more. Soon, very soon, nothing would ever hurt the four of them again.

Brenny stumbled down the cliff path; Jace staggered in his arms. 'Oh, come on, Jace! Come on!'

He'd had to lift his brother on to the window-sill. Jace had fought at first, but then he'd seemed to help a little. Brenny had let his brother go and the heavy body had tumbled outside on to the grass. Jace had groaned and Brenny, for a horrified moment, thought he'd broken his neck. The fall had stirred Jace a bit and although he seemed incapable of speech, he'd been able to take a few stumbling steps, supported by his brother's strength. Brenny hung in close to the cliff wall, pushing Jace against it with all his might. On his right, the sea crashed, and that sound, once so inviting, now had the terror of nightmare in his ears. Jace had once or twice fallen against him so hard that for seconds Brenny had imagined the pair of them falling, falling to the black rocks. Would they die straight away or would the sharks come in the black water and tear them to pieces? He thought of his mother and he thought of God. 'God,' he said aloud, 'please do not let us fall. And please send Mum.' But God, as Brenny well knew, was contrary. Little kids died a lot. In car crashes, in hospitals, in their own beds. Maybe, he thought as he rested briefly, they were real bad kids, or kids that God knew would grow up to be like Hitler. But why hadn't God put Hitler in a car crash?

He sat for a second beside the still figure of his brother. A thin mist had come up and he was suddenly shivering with cold. He hadn't done anything really bad. Neither had Jace. But then he remembered wishing his father dead the night he was screaming at Mum and pushing her around. And Sharmers was still back in that bedroom. The fear shoved him along. He bullied his brother to his feet. Jace groaned. They mustn't die. They mustn't.

The roar of the waves rang horribly loud now. He put out his hand to where the soldiers' house should be. Nothing. Just cool, misty air. Blurred stars shone down as Brenny started to cry. He couldn't be lost. With Jace staggering and falling against him, he edged down the blind path. His questing hand knocked sharply against something hard and smooth. He let Jace slip to the ground and patted with open palms. They were there! He edged around to the front, trying to work out the safest way of getting Jace there. He returned to the snoring figure of his twin, nearly tripping over him in the darkness.

'Come on, Jacey. Help me a bit. *Come on!*' The desperate command in Brenny's voice penetrated Jace's stupefied brain. He staggered in his brother's arms and they made their painful way to the threshold. It was cold in there, and very black. Then Brenny patted his brother. He stepped out and made his way back up the cliff path, full of fear for Charmaine, himself and his brother.

Lisa slowly stood. She broke the gun and pushed two cartridges home. The golden bases shone in the kitchen's dim light. She stood awhile. The sleeping pills would have worked well and truly now, she thought. Her beautiful children would feel no pain; they would simply sleep for ever. She was startled by a sound from the bedroom, a thump. There was a silence again. She sat slowly. Time enough. She could wait a little longer. She must not add to the world's huge burden of pain and fear. She must not be cruel like the soldiers and the lions, or the shooters. Finally, she thought, I am the Snow Queen, frozen and stately, numb to human sorrows. Ice-blue, she whispered to herself. I am ice-blue. Inside me, the whirlpool has stopped, frozen solid, millions of degrees below, a huge spiral of ice.

Brenny crushed Charmaine to him in terror. Blindly, he tried to swing her heavy body off the window-sill. But she lolled like a puppet and his arms were drained from hauling Jace so long that she rolled away from him and fell back inside the bedroom. He blundered away into the darkness and remembered that just in front of him was the menace of the cliff. He tacked sideways, trying to find the scrubby bitou bush that grew in clumps near the edge of the precipice. Sharmers had eaten its flowers only yesterday. He groped around but felt nothing. The roar of the sea terrified him now. Brenny fell to his knees, crawling around desperately. Behind him, from the house, he could hear Lisa yelling, but the new wind, the crash of the sea and the beating in his own head deafened him. He crawled face first into a bush that hurt his eyes. But he didn't cry. He'd found the low green clumps. He tried to force a way into it, but it clung to him, not letting him through. He started ripping at it until he had torn a desperate path into its heart. Finally he stopped. Every part of him hurt. His hands were sticky with blood and there were sore bits all over him. He couldn't look anywhere, nor turn his head at all for the pressure of the branches against his body.

Then he heard what Lisa was saying. In the relative silence between the toppling of the waves, he could hear her voice. 'Come back, Brenny. Come back!' Her voice didn't sound too far away and Brenny trembled to think of the mess he'd made breaking into the bush, and how easy it would be for her to follow him. 'Please, please, come back. The last thing I want to do is hurt you.'

Brenny stiffened. There. She'd admitted it. He sat very still, pressed on all sides by bruising stems and branches. She'd admitted it at last. He started to sob silently, for himself, for Jace and for Sharmers, because he hadn't been able to save his baby and soon, surely, it would start getting light and Lisa would find him.

Lisa picked up Charmaine from where she lay against the wall. She'd put the gun on a bed and she cradled the child tenderly. She didn't notice the cool, limp hands that trailed, nor the faint blueness around Charmaine's parted lips.

'Sharmers, darling Sharmers,' she crooned. She heard nothing as six men positioned themselves around the house, getting into a wide circle, training binoculars through every window. All was quiet. It didn't seem to matter to her that she'd lost the boys. Sharmers was the most precious.

136

Tom Bennett and Verity sat in the police car, well back from the house.

'Bev Hennessy wants to come, but we can't allow that. It's the very worst thing to do in situations like this. It's you she wants.'

'Yes. I know that.'

'When we get there, I want you to approach the house. Will you do that? Just get her talking. Talk about anything. Anything she wants to. Promise her anything. Just talk. She might very well walk into your arms. I'll talk to the blokes here and see what's been happening.'

'Tom?'

'Yes?'

'What if she's done it?'

Tom Bennett didn't answer, just squeezed her arm.

A whisper from the dark. 'Detective Sergeant Bennett?'

'Yes. What is it?'

'The juvenile is armed. An old double-barrelled shot-gun. She's got a baby with her. No sign of the other two kids. But they might be in one of the bedrooms.'

'Christ!'

'She's not doing much. Just wandering around with the baby.'

Bennett turned to Verity.

'Will you? Will you go up now? I'll go round the back. Jack, Mrs Unicombe is going to approach the juvenile and try to talk. I'll try and get the child away if circumstances permit.' The other policeman melted away.

'I'm scared,' whispered Verity, amazed at the paucity of the words. She was feeling blocked: terror, hope, love, fear and something that ached.

'You bet,' he whispered back. 'just do what comes naturally.'

And he was gone.

Verity crept up to the back veranda. She turned to look behind her. She could see nothing; just a dimness where the road cut through the blackness of the trees. The surge and swing of the Pacific was all she could hear. She stood still and breathed deeply and tried to steady herself. Lisa. Jumbo. The juvenile. Another Perdita. Here she was at last. The beginning of the end of a long, long journey. She knocked softly on the door.

'Lisa? It's me. Mrs Unicombe.'

There was no answer. She tried again, louder. Cautiously, she looked round the corner of the back door. She stepped on to the veranda and then into the kitchen. The house was completely still, her own breathing the only sound. A spilled box of ammunition on the floor made her freeze and stare. When she could, she crept through into the lounge room. She noticed the Christmas decorations with a pang; the clothes-peg fairy on the tree; the fancy streamers and chains of stars; even the reindeer cut from folded paper that hung from the mantelpiece was hers. He only had one antler; that part was always tricky. Almost all of her Christmas-craft lessons were hanging before her eyes. She blinked quickly, unprepared for this terrible sadness.

'Lisa?'

Still no answer. But then, a door off the lounge room slowly opened. Lisa Brand stood there, Charmaine in her arms, mixed up and cradled with the shot-gun.

'The Unicorn. You came.'

The girl seemed to sway, or was it, Verity thought, the blurring of her own eyes? The two stood, regarding each other. Time stopped and even the Pacific seemed to pause.

'How are you, Lisa?' What a stupid, stupid thing to say, thought Verity. But a slow smile moved the girl's dilated eyes.

'Me? Oh, I'm fine. Just fine. You really came. You did care?

'Yes.'

Verity allowed her eyes to leave the girl's. Slowly they travelled to the baby and Verity stiffened, trying not to let her fear show.

'Lisa. Why not give me the baby to hold?'

But Lisa, sensitive as a dog, had smelt the woman's terror.

'No. No.' She retreated, clutching the small body close to her. 'You mustn't take her.'

'But, Lisa, look at her. She needs help. She might need a doctor.'

Lisa shook her head. She looked trapped. Oh God, Verity thought, I'm doing everything wrong. I'm pressuring her.

Lisa was crying.

'It all went wrong. I made them frightened. I made the world more dreadful. I caused more pain.'

Verity said nothing. She dared not ask about the boys.

'The boys are gone,' Lisa was saying. 'Gone.'

'Look,' said Verity, 'let's sit down and have a talk. I'll make you a coffee. I would have answered your first letter but I lost the address. Can we talk now?'

Again the retreat, the step backwards. Verity pretended not to notice.

'Or,' she continued, 'you could make the coffee. You know where everything is.'

Lisa looked at her carefully. Very slowly, she put Charmaine down on a chair. She still clutched the gun even though the weight and awkwardness of it was burdensome to her. It was an extraordinary and awesome sight, Verity thought, to see the slim young girl putting the jug on with one hand. Verity edged closer to the still form of the baby. But Lisa swung on her.

'No! Don't touch Sharmers, please.' There was a desperate edge to the voice.

'Of course I won't if you'd rather I didn't.'

Lisa poured a cup of instant coffee.

'Aren't you having one?'

'No.' She looked at Verity. 'And there's no milk left.'

'That's fine. I like it black.'

Verity took the cup and slowly sat on a deep old-fashioned armchair. For the first time since she'd been inside this house, she was feeling there was a chance. She no longer felt the horror and sadness that had assailed her as she walked through the bare rooms. She was sitting, quite comfortably, sipping weak black coffee and one of her ex-pupils was

139

crouched in a chair opposite her. A still baby lay across Lisa's lap. Yes, Verity told herself, the situation can be redeemed if I keep my head. But what had the girl meant by saying the boys were gone? Dear God, she prayed, don't let them be dead. She tried to steady a shaking hand as she raised the coffee to her lips. Lisa's hunched appearance opposite her suggested an inner collapse, as if her spirit had already fled and only a shell of slight humanity was left. A sound from outside and Verity froze while Lisa clutched the gun with white fingers.

'What was that?'

'I don't know. A tree? The house?'

'It wasn't the house.' Lisa's eyes narrowed. 'Did you bring anyone with you?'

'No. No.' Did the girl notice the lying, panicky edge to her voice? 'No. I came alone. My husband's away.' The truth of that statement softened her tone, gave her confidence.

'How did you find me?'

Verity considered a moment. 'I went to your parents' place.'

Lisa turned her face away and her voice was barely audible. 'How were they?'

'They were—well—they were very worried. They know you love the kids. They know you wouldn't hurt them for the world.' Was that the right thing to say, Verity wondered. Then it occurred to her with sickening clarity just where she was and what was happening in this house. She just had time to put the coffee down before she dropped it. I might be almost dead, she was thinking. I might be minutes—seconds away from ceasing to exist. I must tell her. I must make my confession.

'Lisa. There's something I have to tell you. No one else really knows.'

The urgency of the teacher's voice touched the drugged despair of the girl. Lisa turned towards her. 'What?'

'Sixteen years ago—it will be exactly to the day tomorrow —I had a baby, a beautiful girl. But I wasn't married. I was only nineteen then, and nineteen then was like sixteen now. I didn't know what to do. So I let them take my daughter. I gave her up for adoption. I thought I wouldn't be able to care for her properly. I was very sad. It all seemed too much for me. But I thought that if I gave her to a good family, a family who'd love her, she'd be better off than if she stayed with me.' She continued, keeping her voice very low. 'I can remember thinking everything was hopeless. I know what it's like to think that there's no point to anything. That the world is a terrible place. Believe me, I know.'

'What *is* the point?' The voice was sullen and hopeless. 'Why do terrible things happen? And why does everything hurt so much?'

Verity thought deeply. She shook her head. 'I just don't know the answers to those questions. We all hurt, one way or another. But you mustn't lose sight of the beautiful things.'

'How can you lose sight of something that isn't there?'

Careful, thought Verity. Don't argue. She shook her head. 'Sometimes you can't see anything that isn't sad and cruel and dreadful. That's true. But sometimes, the terrible things get so big that they block out your view of other things. That's happened to me.'

But Lisa's face had sagged and her pallor was alarming, matching that of the child that lay against her. Lisa spoke again, very softly. 'Your baby. Did you miss her?'

'Very much. All my life.' Verity felt unshed tears push behind her eyes. 'All my life,' she repeated. 'I don't think a day's gone by that I haven't hurt to think of her—wish that she was with me. But I have to try and forgive myself. I was only a silly girl. I did what I thought was best. That's why I feel so concerned about you. You're the same age as my girl. You're suffering. I do want to help you, Lisa.'

In the silence where the sound of the sea swelled and faded monotonously, Verity thought she saw the girl's face shift. 'Do you only care about me because of your daughter?'

How to explain, Verity thought? How to make Lisa understand that, yes, that was a large part of it; but that that in no way detracted from Lisa's unique value. It was only through being able to make the leap from self to other that we can learn to love at all. She spoke simply.

'I care for you, Jumbo, because you're you.'

Lisa sighed deeply, or perhaps she simply adjusted the weight of the heavy baby on her lap.

'Did you want to be dead?'

Verity considered. Her despair of nearly sixteen years ago had festered into a dull ulcer.

'I did. Yes. But it passed.'

Lisa didn't answer for a while. Then her eyes, eloquent with misery, looked into Verity's own.

'I love these kids. I've thought and thought. I've had rats running round my mind for weeks. I wanted to keep them safe.'

Verity stiffened with excitement. 'I wanted,' the girl had said. Was she changing her mind? Or, most ominous, was she speaking of herself as if she were already dead?

'Will you give me the baby, now, Lisa?' Lisa looked searchingly into Verity's eyes. Verity continued in the low, intimate voice. 'She might need help.'

Lisa gave no indication of having heard her. 'I wanted to save her from knowing all the terrible things.'

'I know you did. I understand that. But as well as terrible things, there are things beautiful beyond belief. She'll grow up to enjoy them. And the boys, too. And so will you. I'll do everything in my power to help you.'

Was Lisa nodding? It was hard to tell. It might have been just that her sad head had moved forward in despair. Slowly, the girl gathered the still form of Charmaine into her arms. She hugged and kissed the child, smoothing her hair. The gun lay neglected beside her. Thank God, Verity thought, in rusty prayer. Slowly she stood and began to move towards Lisa.

Wrong, terribly wrong. Lisa froze.

'No. Don't come near me. I'll bring her in a minute. Don't come near me.'

Later, when Verity recalled those last few words and the mood in that house, she was to remember how a silence, like a spell, had seemed to envelop them, and that with the eerie silence had come another bewitchment, that of immobility. She stood quite still and looked at Lisa who held the child with the gun beside her, a paradoxical tableau. Perhaps it was her own intense concentration that had deafened her to the sounds of the sea or to any other sound that might have warned her; given her a chance to act somehow. Or was it, she thought, the extraordinary intimacy they'd achieved, as formal as it was real, the measured frankness of their mutual confessional?

Then Lisa repeated her command, 'Don't come near me.'

Or was it a plea? Was she afraid Verity might pierce the ice that froze her and drag her back to painful life? Verity took another step towards the girl and suddenly Tom Bennett materialized in the room. Verity stiffened, looked in horror, as if what was unfolding in those following seconds, were a dreadful rehearsal of what might happen if she didn't act. Immobilized, she watched as Lisa dropped the child onto the couch, and grabbed the shotgun. Tom Bennett froze midstride, attempted to say something, but his urgent tones were drowned by Lisa's shriek. Tom sprang towards the girl who leaped backwards in terror. Then came a deafening roar and Tom Bennett crashed backwards bloodily across the room. In the shocking silence that followed the ringing of the gunshot, the sound of the sea filled Verity's ears as she stood in the room, as still and silent as the crumpled body of the man.

Brenny woke from his doze to the sound of the gun. Oh, no, he wept. Sharmers, my baby. If only he'd been big enough, brave enough to get her out. He rocked to and fro in his grief, unmindful of the sharp stems that pierced him.

Verity's hands flew to her face. This did not really happen, a voice said. This is not real. She couldn't scream. Couldn't think. She stood staring. At the figure of the girl who still had the shot-gun levelled ahead of her, face drained, eyes brilliant. Then, as Verity watched, Lisa seemed to collapse in slow motion to her knees. The gun fell heavily beside her. 'Oh, no,' the girl was moaning, 'oh, no. Oh, God.'

Verity slowly turned her eyes to where Tom Bennett was lying, in the corner, his face mercifully downwards and utterly still. She was blind with shock. The room had darkened; she couldn't see properly; her field of vision had narrowed to two keyholes. She didn't know how long things went on like that; the girl moaning, the Pacific surging below, the partial blinding of her vision. In her head, a silly little voice started to say, 'She just shot him, she just shot him,' a little monkey voice until she could bear it no longer.

'Lisa!' she cried.

The girl grabbed the gun as if a spell had been broken. She screamed, 'Look! Look what you made me do! You tricked me! You brought him with you! You lied to me. You didn't care at all! You didn't care for me at all!'

Verity shook her head, as much to clear it as to deny the charges. Talk, poor Tom Bennett had said. Just talk.

'Lisa. I did care. I do care. He came because of the children. He didn't come to get you. He wanted to save the children.' The lie sounded pathetic but Lisa's eyes fixed on hers. 'The children's mother, Lisa. She was very worried. You can understand that.'

Lisa nodded. 'He wanted to save. the children,' she repeated in a whisper. 'I can understand that.' Two tears coursed down her face.

'Lisa. Please come. Let's go home. Let's go now.'

There was a silence. Verity was screaming inside, 'Where are you, where are you, bloody police? What's happening now?' But Lisa shook her head.

'No. I can never go home. Nothing matters any more. I wanted things to be beautiful for them. I wanted to save them from all the pain. But I only made it worse. I frightened and hurt them. I added to the pain in the world—the thick black thing.'

'What do you mean?'

But Lisa didn't answer. She stood there, sagging, with the gun beside her.

'Lisa. Let me take the baby and go. Please, Lisa. You can think then. Let me take the baby.' Cautiously, Verity moved closer.

But Lisa shook her head.

'No. Stay here. I want you here.'

Verity felt tears of hopeless defeat sting her eyes. In the corner, the body of Tom Bennett seemed oddly diminished and not at all real; like a piece of theatre badly done. Even the baby now looked like a mere doll. The only two real things were Lisa and herself. A sudden distorted noise shocked them both. For a horrible moment, Verity thought the dead man on the floor was attempting to find his shattered voice.

'This is Detective Jack Lawrence speaking. Let Mrs Unicombe and the child leave the house. We will not hurt you, Lisa.'

Lisa froze. Verity plunged on without considering.

'There's six of them out there, Lisa. Do as they say. Let's not—let's not get anyone else hurt.'

'Hurt?' Lisa's drugged eyes looked puzzled. 'How could they hurt me any more? I hate myself. I want to die. Hurt?'

Verity felt her legs go under her. What do you do, she was thinking, with such naked anguish? Where does the comfort —what comfort?—come from? In the girl's eyes she had glimpsed such a desolation, such a wintry waste of despair, that she herself could not imagine, nor bear the thought of enduring. She fell back on to the chair, her legs finished with the burden of holding her upright. Her eyes fixed on the child that lay so silent on the old sofa. She covered her face and despaired. And so for a time they sat, on and on, the only sound the surge of the sea. Lisa's blindness seemed only to respond to the slightest movement on Verity's part; a turning of the head, a tightening up, a glance from the dead eyes.

But talk, Tom Bennett had said. Aware of some sacred duty to be performed for the recently dead, Verity tried. She talked of school, of her students, of the day that both she and Lisa remembered now so well.

'It was a beautiful hanky.'

'It was a present from Helen—Miss Bradshaw. You remember her.'

Lisa nodded. 'She was nice.'

Sometimes Verity thought the girl was going to die under her eyes. Or was she merely fainting? She kept herself talking, her voice low and monotonous like a mantra, saying mad things, jumbled things, any silly, crazy thing that drifted into her shocked and despairing mind. But any movement was met with that lifting of the glance, that tightening of the fingers on the gun. Verity, behind the ramblings, tried to think of how she could scoop up the child and be out through the door. But every time she rehearsed it, it fell apart in fragments as she felt the explosion through her backbone. And this might be her own girl, she was thinking. Would it have added some magic sensitivity, the bond of motherhood? Would she have known automatically the best way to respond?

'Lisa,' she heard herself say, 'Lisa, how can I help you?'

The loud-hailer voice bellowed again and they both jumped. Verity looked at Lisa.

'Let me talk to them. I'll ask them to go away and then we can just go home. They'll go, Lisa, if I ask them.'

Lisa made no answer. Very cautiously, and holding Lisa's eyes with her own as long as she could, Verity walked slowly to the window. She raised her clear teacher's voice.

'Please, gentlemen, will you go away? Lisa will come with me. Lisa and the baby. Please go away.'

There was no answer for a minute. Then, 'This is Lawrence, Mrs Unicombe. We're going now.' Then there was silence.

'Do you think they've gone?'

Verity tried to feel the tone in the question. Was it conspiratorial or despairing?

'I'm sure they have. We can go safely now. Shall I carry the baby?'

And Lisa nodded. Verity picked up the heavy baby. Oh

baby, she said to herself, how limp and pale you are. 'Shall we go now?'

'You go, Mrs Unicombe. I'll stay here.'

Verity shrank from the implication. 'No. You come with me. I'm taking you home, remember?' But the girl resisted.

'You come home with me,' Verity continued. 'There's no one there but me.' And the ghosts, and the ghosts, she thought. But Lisa shook her head. She raised her eyes to Verity's and Verity thought of Medusa and that if she had done more than merely glimpse the waste of hell in those eyes she would have been stone for ever.

'Lisa. My poor child.'

Slowly, she turned away, cuddling the baby close to her. Then she felt a tentative, cold hand on her arm.

'Mrs Unicombe, give me Sharmers. Let me hold her one more time.'

Verity was torn. She was loathe to relinquish the baby. But she thought of Tom Bennett. She looked at the baby's still face. Her mind was in turmoil. Talk, she remembered. Talk. Agree with anything she says.

'Of course, Lisa. If you really want to. But look at her. She's sick. She needs help. Don't you think I should get her to the hospital as soon as I can?'

Lisa covered her face. 'I did that to her. I gave her sleeping tablets. And Brenny. And Jace. I didn't want them to be frightened. But it all went wrong.'

Verity clutched the baby tightly. Charmaine might be dead or dying in her arms this very moment.

'I'm sure she'll be all right. And the boys. Where are they?'

'I don't know. I don't know what happened. It all went wrong.'

Verity feared to pressure her. 'Perhaps I'd better go now.'

At that moment, Jack Lawrence, a hundred yards away, leaned across the front seat of his car to adjust the radio and bumped the horn. He swore and jumped away but not before its harsh call had blared for a fraction of a second through the stillness.

147

Lisa recovered first from the shock. She sprang forward and grabbed Charmaine from Verity's unresisting arms and vanished from the house.

'Oh Jesus!' Lawrence cried. One of the others yelled out, 'She's run out with the kid!' and then he was sprinting forward as the high-powered lights hit the shabby house. But the house blocked the radiance on the other side and the girl knew the path. He had only his torch in that dark blackness.

Verity ran to him. 'Over there! She went over there!'

'Where does it go to?'

'I don't know.'

And then a small figure came running and crying to them, clutching the front of his pyjamas.

'She's got my baby. She's taking her down there.'

Verity ran to Brenny. The little boy was shivering and his terrified face shocked her. She tried to pick him up but his rigid body prevented her.

'Jace's down there where she's gone. In the soldiers' house.' He began to whimper.

'Don't worry now. It's all right. You go back and get into one of the cars.' But Brenny wouldn't yield.

'She'll get Sharmers. And Jace.'

'No. I'm sure they'll be safe now.'

'She gave them red drink with stuff in it. I threw mine away.'

One of the police officers scooped the child up in his arms. The others followed Lawrence down the cliff path, and Verity, hardly knowing what she did, stumbled after them.

Lisa stood at the edge, near the top of the cliff and east of the path. A little while ago, she'd seen the torches and the shouting men winding down past her, to the beach, where they spread out, their small lights dancing on the hidden sand and surf. She hugged Charmaine to her. Even if she hadn't been able to save the boys, she could still save Sharmers, the most precious of all. Below her, the great sea sang and the horrors that had haunted her for so long seemed very far away. The night was veiled, and a cold moon shone now through misty air. She stood on the cliff's edge and looked at the pale circle in the sky with its ghostly aura haloed around it.

Verity had fallen back behind the searchers, unable to keep up the pace. She stopped feeling her way and shivered at the thought of the rocks. The horror of the night, her exhaustion and her shock were all telling on her. She found she couldn't take another step. The shivering increased until her whole body was knocking against itself. She hung on to a clump of sharp-sided grass, as if to let it go would mean a plunge into hell.

The racking eased and she looked east, out to the invisible sea. Not twenty yards away stood a slight figure, just discernible in the wan light. Verity prayed. Please. Not in front of my eyes. Please. But the figure remained quite still. Verity tried a final rally. She moved closer to the girl. When she was almost behind her, she spoke in a low and shaking voice.

'Lisa. I understand. I understand what you meant. That you meant to save them from the pain. But there is only pain because you love, and without love we shrivel.' The girl said nothing. Verity was silent, too. She was finished, drained utterly.

Lisa remained as if she hadn't heard. But the words had come through and she was starting to feel again. The numbness of the last hours was fading; she was being filled again with turmoil and anguish. The ditch people screamed and ran, trying to hide, the zebra lifted its dying head and the kangaroo gleamed wet and raw again. Tom Bennett died over and over; the horror of his going frozen on his face. She had done nothing but add to the suffering. Lisa threw back her head and howled to the moon-filled sky.

'Stop it! Stop it!'

And in one movement, the more awesome because of its terrible grace, Lisa turned, thrust the child into Verity's arms and stepped forward into darkness. Verity buried her face in the child's soft body. There was no sound, no sound to come back and haunt her memory. Just a terrible aching sense of loss and the wash of the waves, ever returning.

17

After the final interviews with the police, the questions, the exhaustion, Verity found that shock was not the merciful buffer she had heard about. The very confusion it created only added to her turmoil. Helen helped her through the ordeal, reformulating the detectives' questions, prompting replies, translating, it seemed, from a foreign language. Her friend offered to stay with her for a day or two, but Verity longed for peace and to be alone. When Richard rang she told him she was fine and begged him not to cut short his holiday. She hung up and looked around the lounge room, now unfamiliar to her, trying to feel that she was at home.

The next few days, thought Verity later, were the worst of her life. It was as if pain was the only teacher in this world; one either went under or lived through it and learned from it. The memories of earlier griefs were eclipsed; trivialized by the intensity of now's pain and fear. Whenever she thought she could feel no more suffering, some new, fresh ambush of misery seized her.

She would wake from fitful sleep to lie in bed and stare as the hot sun crept up the wall. She would finally shower and dress, moving mechanically, empty of spirit. She would deliberately make and butter toast, and then let it congeal as she watched it. Food nauseated her; her turmoil filled her head until she thought she would have to break her skull open. She would rock herself, staring at the pale carpet. Once, she found herself banging her head hopelessly against the wall. This is too much, she whispered. This burden is too much for me to bear. Rats running round the brain, the girl had said. But these aren't rats. These are huge, flesh-tearing creatures that tear me night and day. Sleep was impossible without drugs.

She'd pace the house, chain-smoking. Why? she'd ask. Why did it happen? That good man blown into nothingness. That poor child. For what reason? Me, she would answer. I caused it by my lack of love. Up and down, she went, like a caged carnivore, turning on the same spot until the carpet was hot under her feet with the friction of her desperate passing. So caught up, I was, with my own pain, I couldn't hear the voice of another's anguish. That first letter. If I'd answered that first letter, none of this would have happened. At two or three o'clock in the morning, she'd sometimes collapse drunk on the couch, to wake as the sun streamed across her an hour or so later. Hideous images tormented her, waking or sleeping. The death of Tom Bennett, the imagined explosion of Lisa's body on the rocks below; carrion sharks tearing the young limbs; the ice-blue sea blackened with clouds of blood. Verity felt as if she had unlimited credit on the world's store of horror and pain, to be drawn on constantly, spent immediately, re-earned and recredited to that hellish account.

Sunlight sickened her like a vampire. Once she tried to eat, but vomited the barely chewed food into the sink and let it lie there. So she drank whisky instead of eating. Helen's number didn't answer. She noticed without interest that she could no longer take a bath; her tail bones were too sharp and painful against the enamelled surfaces. She stopped washing. She cared nothing for her appearance. Only one thing continually fascinated her; that such anguish could be experienced and she still did not die. She touched a cigarette to her wrist and the physical pain seemed a relief, filling her mind with its sharpness. If I could burn all the time, she thought to herself, I wouldn't hurt so much.

She drank herself into oblivion every day. The ugly spirits blurred the pain. But she knew, too, that they were assisting her collapse. 'Large quantities,' she heard herself say aloud one morning, 'of a toxic depressant is probably not a good idea at the moment. So let's have another one.' She laughed at this bitterness and almost fell. 'My spirit is dying,' she said, 'so I must replace my spirit.' She poured another one. Odd bits and pieces of poetry came to mind and, Ophelia-like, she quoted them in jumbles. It was good to know, at last, she thought, that Lisa was right. This world and all its pain is too dreadful. And all of it is crammed into this up here. She tapped her forehead. All of it. Somehow magically concentrated inside this tiny sphere of bone; distilled and perfected into purest anguish. It should be spouting out of my ears, my nose, my eyes, she thought, like an evil stinking liquid. What a hideous miracle, that this tiny ball at the end of my neck can contain all this all the time. Mrs Atlas, she thought to herself, Mrs Atlas of the Sorrows. And poured herself another drink.

Her mad quotations echoed through the empty house as she stumbled around; bits of pop songs, Hopkins or Shakespeare, all together in crazy oddments. 'How can the birds go on singing? / How can the sun shine above? / Don't they know it's the end of the world? / It ended when I lost my love.' Or she announced to the bookshelves, 'I am become Death, Destroyer of Worlds.' She fell, spilling her whisky. She lay on the carpet. 'I am dying, Egypt, dying,' she muttered to the floor that was squashing her lips out of shape—and passed out.

She woke. A skeletal hand was crouched on the carpet in front of her eyes near the overturned glass. 'Ah,' she sighed with relief, 'you've finally come for me, fell sergeant. Into your metacarsels I commit my dead spirit.' And she passed out again.

It was hateful to wake to consciousness later and to find that the hand was only hers. She crawled across to the drink cupboard. A headache was exploding inside her cranium. 'Oh, let it hurt, let it hurt,' she sobbed. 'If it will only hurt enough, I can die.' The only alcohol now left in the cupboard was some green stuff. A present from a kid. Kids, she thought, that's right. I teach kids. She sat back on her heels, considering herself. I am the Unicorn and I teach kids. I give kids away, too. And I cause them to hurl themselves off cliffs.

She reached in for the decorative bottle. She had no idea of the time. It is dark time, she told herself. At the third stroke, it will be dark, twenty-dark and dark seconds. She battled with the bottle top and finally tore it off. She up-ended the green fluid into her mouth. This must stop, a voice from inside the cloud of headache said. This must stop.

The phone was ringing. She ignored it. It stopped, then started again. This time she swayed over to it and struck it off the hook. A pygmy voice squeaked from the handset that dangled on the floor. Then it stopped and the engaged sound filled her ears. She leaned back on her heels, nearly falling. She clutched the bottle to her. 'Help me,' she begged no one in particular. 'Please help me.' She toppled sideways and the sticky drink went with her. She watched it inch viscously across the patch of carpet near her eyes. 'Help me,' she whispered again. 'I can't do it any more.'

Then she was in the convent infirmary; gentle hands were bathing her. A warm cloth was passing tenderly over her body. She could smell the freshness of clean linen, the scent of her heavy roses.

She opened her eyes. The infirmary seemed to be her own bedroom.

'Lie still, darling. Just lie still and let me clean you up a bit.' She followed the hand and the arm up to its shoulder joint. She was in the Infirmary because there was her mother wearing her starched head-dress, or was it just her hair? She closed her eyes again.

'You've been very sick, sweetheart. And Helen sounded so worried when she called,' came her mother's voice from nearby. 'But it's all right now because I'm here to look after you.'

Tears seeped out of Verity's eyes. She shook her head from side to side. She couldn't speak. Her mother anticipated her. 'Don't try to talk. Sleep. You need to sleep and rest yourself. I'm here and I love you.'

Verity nodded and tried to say something then fell asleep.

*

The day before Richard was due back, her mother left. A spring-clean, thought Verity. A summer-clean. She lugged the heavy fabric off the couch and washed it. She washed walls and curtains, scrubbed the bathroom; did what she could about the stains on the carpet. She swept and polished and scrubbed, hoping to exhaust herself into dreamless sleep. But her imagination was relentless and punishing. Over and over it went through the events of that night at the beach house.

A good man dead; a child in despair. If only, she drove herself mad with; if only. It seemed to her that the sum of her life had been a series of pathetic blunders, awesome in their stupidity. Her love affair with the cold academic, the loss of her daughter, her marriage, her bitterness towards her mother.

Her marriage. She and Richard chafed together in their mutual bonds, bonds that seemed sometimes to be entirely made of resentments and loss. Richard. She'd barely thought of him for days. And then when someone had really needed her, and reached out for her, what had she done? Nothing. Such were her feelings as she pulled the fridge away from the wall with a furious tug. When she found the first letter there, she stared at it for a few minutes. Then she read it.

Hi, Miss,
You mightn't remember me. You taught me in 6E3. I've left school now and I can't get a job. I try real hard but there's thousands and thousands of us all going for the same job. Every day is just as bad as every other day. I often think of you because you were a good teacher to me.

Jumbo

And there was Lisa's address clearly printed above the date.
Verity fell to her knees, weeping.

Helen let her in, concern all over her features, all her gestures.

'You can't blame yourself, Verity. You mustn't. Try not to.'

'Try not to breathe, Helen.'

'I know. I know.' She poured them both a stiff drink. Then she sat beside her friend.

'You can't know how things are going to turn out until they do. That sounds stupid. But it's true. A lot of common-place observations are.'

'But, Helen. I should have picked up her despair. "Every day is just as bad as every other day." That is someone in great pain. And it was terrible that night, seeing her like that.' Verity tried to close her eyes against the memory.

'Vee, do you know what I think?' Verity opened her eyes. 'I think Lisa saved the baby because of you. I think that's why she gave it to you before she jumped. Because you'd told her about your girl. Instead of blaming yourself for every-thing, why not see that? She gave you back a baby girl. Charmaine is alive because of you. You didn't cause Tom Bennett's death. He was a brave man doing a job—taking a risk—and he mistimed it. Perhaps if he'd waited a bit longer—you can't take it all on yourself. You're only looking on the worst side, punishing yourself. You are being exactly like Lisa was.'

Verity was shocked. But there was a truth in what Helen was saying. She remembered her own words to Lisa that night; what she'd told her about the beautiful things. She leaned back in her chair and thought about them. Her husband, her garden, her mother, the perfection of certain days, the love and enthusiasm of a responsive class, even her own baby's beauty. Yes. Helen was right. She was being like Lisa.

Richard returned. 'You should have telegrammed me.'

'Why? What was the point? It was all over.'

'Look, Vee. If I'd known.'

'Yes,' she said, but the bitterness was directed at herself and not at him, 'if *I*'d known.'

In bed, she told him, 'I went to see the Brands. They were

hating me, I could tell that. They were perfectly polite. But they were hating me for the fact that she'd written to me. They blame me, too.'

'It's easier for them to do that, rather than examine themselves. You don't have to take the blame, you know.' He put his arms around her. 'I'm so sorry, Vee. I'm so sorry I wasn't here.'

She kissed him and forgave him and they made tender love together.

A little later he spoke again.

'Are you awake?'

'Yes.'

'I'll help you, if you like.'

'How?'

'With your search for your daughter.'

'But you've always been dead set against it.'

'I was frightened.'

'What of?'

She felt his body shrug. 'Not sure.'

She lay awake a long time thinking of Helen's words and of her own words to the unhappy girl. She thought of her mother and was filled with love and gratitude. Odd, she thought to herself, that you select the things that will hurt you the most and then proceed to devote all your waking hours to tormenting yourself with them. Am I some sort of masochist? she asked herself while Richard breathed gently beside her. Why do I carry all this guilt, like Lisa? Why am I so pitiless with myself? What makes me court the blame and the guilt and the pain, from myself, my mother, the Brands? She turned over to cuddle Richard's warm back. I love you, she whispered to him. And I love you, my dear mother. And I love you, too, my lost girl. I can relinquish you. I can accept that you are well and happy with the lovely Catholic couple on the coast. I'll leave you alone, now, and stop hurting myself, and Richard, too, with this useless pain. Now, she thought, I can finally leave my child to Heaven. 'Goodnight, my darling,' she whispered aloud to the unknown daughter. Goodnight and be at peace.

Slowly, she returned to life. She read, cooked meals, visited Helen, bought tampons, put on the stone she'd lost, gardened in the evenings when it wasn't too hot. She knew now in her heart and guts something she'd only known in her head: that we all let each other down. And if we can forgive each other, in so doing we can finally forgive ourselves.

She started working on her new year's school programme as January drew to a close. There was a freshness between herself and Richard, as if they were newly met, yet had heard about each other for many years through friends. They pottered happily enough. The heat seemed to be accumulative; a few degrees from yesterday still lingered to be added to tomorrow. She was working in the relative cool of the lounge on some geography for sixth class when Richard interrupted her.

'About your daughter. What have you decided to do?'

'Nothing.'

'Nothing?' He looked bewildered. But there was no tone of resentment in her voice, so he went over and kissed her.

'I'm going to see Tony for a while. See you later.'

'Bye.'

When the phone rang, she went to answer it, carrying a very full ashtray with her.

'Hello?'

'Is that Verity Unicombe?'

'Yes. Speaking.'

There was a long silence on the other end and Verity was starting to wonder about nuisance calls when the young voice stumbled and continued,

'Mrs Unicombe. It's Vanessa here. Your daughter. Do you remember me?'

Verity dropped the ashtray, and the butts and ash spread wide over the cream wool carpet.